a

I hope you
enjoy this
book.
Melissa Harman 10/23/24

THE
CREW

Melissa Harman

Fulton Books
Meadville, PA

Published by Fulton Books 2024

ISBN 979-8-88982-885-3 (paperback)
ISBN 979-8-88982-886-0 (digital)

Printed in the United States of America

CHAPTER 1

HAVE YOU EVER FELT THAT your entire life was already planned? That since the day you were born, you were told what to wear, who you could be friends with, what schools you were going to, and the type of person you would become? It was as if you were being molded into something you were never meant to be. Well, that's how I feel now. I'm not rich by any means. That's not the lifestyle for me. I'm just a middle-class eighteen-year-old who just graduated high school, the same high school both my parents attended, of course. You would think I would be happy, but nope. I feel like I could burst at any moment! I've never felt that I could do my own thing my way! I've never even had the chance to pick out my own clothing when I go shopping with my mom. I'm just supposed to be a good little girl and do as I'm told. Screw that. It all ends now.

CHAPTER 2

LET ME GIVE YOU SOME background information on my parents. My dad is Brad Wolf. He is an only child, but by mistake. His parents were only dating when they found out his mom was pregnant. His dad left almost immediately. He said he was too young to have the responsibility of being a parent. He was only twenty at the time. So his mom was on her own. His mom wasn't any better. She hid the fact that she was pregnant as long as she could, simply because she was scared and didn't know what to do. Then she decided to run away. Nobody really knows what happened to her during that time. What my dad knows is that after he was born, his mom gave him up. She was also only twenty at the time. My dad wound up in foster care. He had made a promise to himself that no matter what happened, if he had kids, he would never leave them. That's a promise that I truly love.

Then there's my mom, Kate Wolf. When people hear her story, they just laugh because they don't believe it's true. But it is. Honestly, it's a story that I didn't quite believe at first.

My mom came from a big family, a family of eight to be exact. Her parents had six kids. My mom was the third child. She had four brothers and one sister. She had two older brothers who didn't always want anything to do with her, so she kept mostly to herself, at least until her younger sister was born. She was very protective of her. They were best pals. Then came her two younger brothers, who just happened to be identical twins.

It's not what you would have expected. None of the boys were into any sports. They didn't have to be when they had all the freedom they could ever want. They skipped school whenever they felt like it with no real discipline. They would drive anyone's vehicle without asking, even if they weren't old enough to drive. They didn't clean around the house if they didn't feel like it. They could basically do anything, and their parents didn't seem to care. Then after some time passed, my mom noticed that, so she tried some things herself just to see if anything would happen to her. One day, she went into her mom's purse and took $50. Nothing happened. The kids would continue to get away with so much more until one day, her two older brothers would get arrested for breaking and entering and stealing a car.

Once her brothers got arrested, my mom then realized that things had to change, that she had to change her act. She did go to community college. She worked hard to pay for herself. Her two other brothers and sister had no interest in further education after they graduated high school.

People would laugh at this because they just don't believe that any parent would allow their kids to do things like that without caring. But because they did, it caused my mom to be who she is today. She learned discipline in the real world with real consequences. She then promised herself that if she became a parent, she would not allow her kids to get away with such things. She became strict, protective, and loving. Maybe she didn't realize how strict she became with me. But now, it's time to get to my story.

My name is Rachael Wolf. It's finally time for me to break free.

CHAPTER 3

MACKENZIE BLUE HAS BEEN MY best friend for as long as I can remember. Well, since fifth grade, to be exact. I had other friends come and go. My parents felt that certain kids were not good enough to be friends with me. My parents felt that some of them were a bad influence on me. Others just couldn't stand my parents. They just didn't like how strict my parents were, but not Mackenzie. She's been around through thick and thin. Good and bad. We know everything about each other. She's the sister I never had. So when I had my idea, she was the first one I called.

"You're going to do what?" Mackenzie asked.

"I can't keep living like this. I need to take control of my life at some point!" I said.

"Okay, I get that, but not going to college like planned can ruin your future!" Mackenzie exclaimed.

"I never said I'm not going at all. I'll go in time, but now I need a break. I'll pretend to go, but I'll be off doing my own thing," I explained.

"I'm not sure I like this," she said. "I'll side with you, I always do, but this is a whole new level."

"I feel that my parents have had full control of my entire life. Like they had to approve of my friends, approve what I wear. I really don't have much of a social life. I'm surprised that I even have a cell phone!" I said. "Plus, this is my first chance at actual freedom! I just feel that I need to jump on it!" I added.

"Okay, I get it. Do you have an actual plan?"

"Not quite yet. I'm working on it. I will for sure let you know what I decide on."

"Okay. This is crazy though," Mackenzie replied.

"Tell me about it. I gotta go. It's late, and I'm really tired."

"Okay. I'll talk to you tomorrow. Good night," Mackenzie said.

"Good night," I replied.

Mackenzie is right, I thought. *This idea is crazy. To pretend to go to college but really go somewhere else.*

"Where am I going?" I asked myself.

I looked at my phone. It was 11:30 p.m. For now, I'll just get some sleep, but tomorrow is a brand-new day.

CHAPTER 4

THAT NIGHT, MY CRAZY PLAN came to me. I thought about it for a while before I decided to call Mackenzie. I needed to get a lot of details in order first. I also had to act normal in front of my parents so they wouldn't expect anything. Good luck with that. This is a crazy plan that I may or may not regret, but it was now or never.

"Hey, girl! It's almost noon! I thought you would have called by now!" Mackenzie said.

"So much for saying hello." I laughed.

"Hello, Rachael. Is that better?" she asked sarcastically.

"Yes, much better." I laughed again. "So my crazy plan is coming together. I'm gonna need your help though," I continued.

"I'm afraid to ask what kind of help," she said.

"Well, about six months ago, you said you were staying in an apartment right off the college campus. You're still doing that, right?"

"Oh yeah! There's no way I could stay in those tiny but expensive dorm rooms! Why?"

"Well, I was thinking about staying with you for the school year. That way, I'll be near the campus, so if my parents stop by, they won't suspect anything," I said.

"I wouldn't mind that. There's just one problem. If you don't attend your classes, they might find out about this," she replied.

"I thought about that. I'll just drop them. I'll say I can't start this year, that something came up. The college can't force me to go, and my parents will never know," I said.

"Maybe. This is more than crazy! This isn't like you at all! I'm used to a very well-behaved girl who worked her ass off to be a

6

straight-A student all through high school. Not a high school grad-uate who is about to go off the rails!" She sounded very concerned.

"I'm not about to go off the rails," I said. "I'm just finally doing something for me! I'm finally making my own decisions. I mean, it isn't the greatest decision, I admit, but it could also be very exciting!" I declared.

"If you say so! We just both have a lot of packing to do!" Mackenzie said.

"It's gonna be so awesome! I can't wait!" I shouted.

"Girl, don't blow my ear out!"

"Totally sorry! There's just one more crazy idea," I said.

"Oh no! I don't even want to know if I want to hear this one. Can it be any worse than bailing on college?" she asked. I could tell she was afraid to ask me that.

"Actually, yes. Way worse."

CHAPTER 5

MY SECOND IDEA WAS JUST outright insane! I would be totally shocked if Mackenzie agreed to it! It could be life-changing. Well, maybe. It could end up with some jail time, that's for damn sure. The thoughts that I've been having were just not me at all!

I'm supposed to be a nice girl. Someone who just couldn't be rude to anyone. Someone who was just very reliable. Someone who would set high goals and do anything it took to achieve those goals. Maybe that just wasn't the real me at all. That thought just scared the living hell out of me.

I had a couple of thoughts going through my mind. First, was I in the process of changing into the person I would be for the rest of my life? Will I turn into someone who my parents wouldn't recognize? Second, I needed to plan my second crazy idea. What I needed were some gloves, masks, and weapons. I wanted to know if I could get away with something.

CHAPTER 6

"WHERE ARE YOU OFF TO?" my mom asked. I had just walked into the kitchen, well, half running, hoping I would avoid that question.

"Um, nowhere really. Just off to meet Mackenzie," I replied, which happened to be a total lie.

"Well, I was really hoping that you would stick around the house today. You know, just you, your father, and I. Maybe we could watch a movie or, better yet, go to a movie."

"I really can't, Mom. I promised Mackenzie." Here she goes again, trying to tell me to change my plans so things work out for her.

"Well, she will understand if you cancel. It's better and safer to have you home anyways. Plus, in a few short months, you're going to be off to college, and you can see Mackenzie any time you want unless you're studying. That always comes first."

My mind was telling me to just run out the door and run the errand I was planning on before I changed my mind. Another part of me said to mind my mother and stay home.

"Is it possible to make a deal with you, Mom?" I asked.

My mom just looked at me like she didn't understand the question.

"Well?" I asked.

"Rachael, I can't believe you would ask me something like that. I understand you're eighteen, and you feel that you're an adult now, but—"

"Really?" I interrupted. "I am an adult, for starters. I was just asking a question."

My mom leaned back against the counter.

"I don't like this attitude, little lady."

"You're kidding, right?"

I just took a deep breath. "I'm not giving you an attitude. I just already made plans, and if I don't leave now, I'm going to be late," I said.

My mom just stood there against the counter, glaring at me. It's a look I've seen many times before. It's the look that says, "My house, my rules." *Well, not today*, I thought.

"How about I go see Mackenzie and come back early to watch a movie with you and Dad? Will that work?"

She just kept glaring at me. Then I could see she was considering it, overthinking it was more like it.

"All right," she finally said. "I feel like you're not telling me something though."

"Oh my god, Mom! You and Dad raised me better than that! Or don't you remember?" Before she could say anything, I ran out the back door. If my mom only knew about my plans, she would possibly disown me. What she doesn't know won't hurt her.

CHAPTER 7

I WAS WALKING ON THE sidewalk down my street and heading to a park to meet up with a secret friend. I say secret friend because my parents have no clue who this person is. The plan is for it to stay that way. It's been a secret for six months now. Mackenzie knows, but that's it. She can be trusted.

This secret friend is a guy named Larry Jones. To me, he's very good-looking. He has broad shoulders, he's about six feet tall, and he has nice brown eyes. He's pretty well-built, which is from being on our high school's football team. He also has this charm about him that's hard to explain. He's a damn good listener too. I'm starting to think I have a crush on this guy. Of course, I just know my parents would approve of him.

He was sitting on top of a table when I spotted him. Even from a distance, he was good-looking. When he saw me, he started to walk my way.

"Hey, what's up?" He leaned in for a hug, and I just had to hug him back.

"Well, I wanted to talk to you about something. It's something crazy. Mackenzie doesn't even know about it yet."

"If she doesn't know about it, then it must be crazy." He looked shocked. He knows the two of us tell each other everything, like literally everything.

I called Larry early that morning and told him about my college plan, and he seemed to understand. He didn't find it crazy at all. It was comforting. He's taking a year off himself.

"Well, lately, I haven't been thinking like myself," I started. I was looking at the ground. I was nervous at this point. "The college idea is one thing. This other plan is just not like me at all."

"Hey," he said, "you can tell me. I won't judge you. Maybe I can even help."

"I was raised to be this perfect person. I never had a job because my parents wanted me to focus on school, which I did. I got all straight As. There was a ton of pressure on me too. Now that school is over, I felt this huge weight just fall off my shoulders." I continued, "It's like I have all this freedom now, and I'm not sure what to do with it, I guess."

"So now you're just not sure what to do?" Larry asked.

"It's just not that. I feel like I need to break free from my parents," I said.

"I can understand that. We all feel that at some point," he said.

"Right. I kind of feel that the things that I'm thinking of doing now are my way of figuring out who I'm supposed to be. It's confusing, and I can't understand it now," I said, now making eye contact with Larry.

"I'll do whatever I can do to help," he said, placing a hand on my arm. "Just tell me about the other idea you have."

"Well, it's pushing the limits a bit. I never had the chance to really get in trouble. I kind of want to know what I can get away with." Then I told him my plan.

He looked at me and just started laughing.

"What's so funny?" I asked, annoyed.

"I'm sorry. It's just kind of funny. I can for sure help you with that."

"Really? How?" I asked.

"I know just the guy."

CHAPTER 8

"YOU GUYS ARE NUTS. YOU do know that, right?" Mackenzie somewhat shouted.

"Take it down a notch or two, will you?" I said.

Larry, Mackenzie, and I were all having lunch at Taco Bell to fill Mackenzie in on what Larry and I had discussed two days earlier at the park.

"Okay, okay," she said, taking a deep breath. "But a convenience store?"

"My boss is totally unreliable. He has this coming. He's had this coming for a long time," Larry whispered.

"Okay, I get how bosses can be total assholes, but robbing them is not the solution," Mackenzie said, shaking her head.

"Should we really be talking about this in public?" I asked.

"Look around, Rachael," Larry said. "We're the only ones here."

"I know, but still. Maybe an employee might hear us," I said, looking over my shoulder.

"Rachael, you're nervous. I get it. This isn't you. Maybe this will be a thrill for you. You know something you need to get out of your system." Larry smiled.

"Really? A thrill? Is that what you're calling it?" Mackenzie asked. She was still a little paranoid, which was to be expected.

"Aren't you supposed to be a nice guy? You know a guy who is supposed to stay out of trouble?" Mackenzie asked.

"Usually, I am. I'm just ready to see this thing through, is all. I just can't be directly involved, is all."

"And why not?" I asked.

13

"If I'm part of this, I will be busted for sure. My boss would for sure recognize my voice. Besides, I would be the first person he would suspect. We don't get along," Larry said.

"Then why not just quit? That would be a lot easier." Mackenzie said.

"I can't. I promised my parents that I would work there until I went to college. Just to prove that I can hold a job."

We all just got quiet. We all just sat there staring at whatever leftovers we had. Was this something that I really wanted to do? I thought. This was my crazy idea after all, wasn't it?

So after what seemed like forever, I finally spoke up, "Okay, so I know I've said I've felt trapped by my parents and that I need to do my own thing. I know that this is illegal, but maybe Larry is right. Maybe it will be a thrill. I know I can use that in my life right now. So screw it. I'm in. Who's with me?"

Larry and Mackenzie looked at each other, and both nodded.

"I'm in," they said in unison.

CHAPTER 9

SO I WAS GOING TO rob a convenience store. Speedway, to be exact. The plan was to wait until Larry's boss, Chuck, was working alone. Then we would make our move. Larry said that there should always be two people there at all times for safety reasons, but his boss was a total dick and didn't care about that. I've never had a job, so I didn't know if that kind of thing is illegal or not, but Chuck will definitely learn the hard way about that soon enough.

It would be on a Monday night after Larry got off work. He would be off at 10:00 p.m., right at closing. Then his boss would be alone with all the money exposed. We knew the doors would be locked, but we had a way around that. Larry had promised that he would make sure he left a door unlocked for us. Larry also said that the safe should be open and that Chuck would have to collect all that money too. This kept getting more exciting and nerve-racking at the same time.

There were a few more things we had to get into order first. We would need all dark clothing, masks, and probably some sort of weapons.

"We could always use pepper spray," Mackenzie said. "That way, we wouldn't be waving guns around."

"That's not a bad idea. I would rather not use a gun. It would probably attract too much attention," I said.

Mackenzie and I were at my house, sitting on my bed and trying to put the pieces of the plan together.

"What about pocketknives? They could come in handy too," she said.

"That's a good idea. I can't believe I'm saying this, but we need a list of things that we need in order to pull this off."

"Got it." I got off the bed, went to my dresser, and got a notebook and pen.

"All right, what's first?" I asked, ready to write.

"All black clothes. Like solid black. It would be easier to hide if we need to for any reason," she said.

"Check." I wrote down all solid black clothes.

"Next, we need masks. I think solid black ski masks would be perfect," she continued.

"Check," I replied.

We continued this until we felt comfortable that we had all our bases covered. We got solid black clothing, black ski masks, thin black gloves so we can move our fingers easily and hopefully don't leave fingerprints behind, two cans of pepper spray, two pocketknives, solid black shoes, and, of course, a bag for the money.

"Are we missing anything?" she asked.

"How am I supposed to know? This is a first for me!" I just started laughing.

"Oh, sure. Laugh now. I bet when the time comes, you won't think it's so funny. You might freeze in place." She sounded kind of serious.

"I know. I'm scared. Laughing just helps, I guess," I said. Right then, someone knocked on my door. Mackenzie and I looked at each other in alarm. We had "oh shit" looks on our faces. I quickly hid the notebook under my pillow.

"Who's there?" I asked.

"Just me," my dad said, slowly opening the door. "How's everything going in here?"

"It's fine," I said.

"Okay. Just checking. You can never be too sure," he said.

"We're totally fine, Mr. Wolf," Mackenzie said. She very rarely calls my parents by their first names. She said it was more respectful to say Mr. and Mrs. Wolf.

"If you girls need anything, just let me know," he said.

"Okay," I replied.

When the door was firmly closed, we were both able to relax.

"Do you think he heard anything?"

"No. If he did, I would know. He would be totally freaking out!"

"I thought we were screwed there for a minute!" We both started laughing then. I reached under my pillow for the notebook. I tore out the sheet that had our list on it, folded it up, and put it in my pocket.

"Better safe than sorry."

CHAPTER 10

"OKAY, SO THIS IS IT," Larry said. "Are you ready?"

"What the hell kind of question is that!?" Mackenzie shot back.

"I get you're nervous, scared, and probably shaky, but I believe you two got this," Larry said.

"I swear I'm gonna break down if the cops show up!" she said.

"There's for sure chance Chuck will call the police. I mean, why wouldn't he?" Larry laughed. Mackenzie leaned over the table and punched him. This time, we were at Mackenzie's house, sitting in the kitchen.

"What? I'm joking! Well, sorta," he said, laughing.

"That doesn't help at all! What do you think, Rachael?" Mackenzie asked.

"No. It's not real comforting," I replied.

"Come on, ladies, lighten up. I'm just trying to have a little fun before the big showdown." He chuckled.

"The big showdown?" I asked.

"Yeah. I just felt like it needed some name. Call it a code name if you want."

"Really? A code name?" Mackenzie said.

"It's better than saying robbery," Larry said.

"Wow! That makes it sound so much worse!" I exclaimed. "I'm a fan of a code name!"

"Let's forget that now and focus," Mackenzie said.

"So it's now 11:30 a.m., and I'll text you when I'm off, then you guys can make your move," Larry said.

"Yeah. We'll be waiting in your car across the street. But we'll pull into the parking lot of McDonald's about ten minutes before you get off, so it's not really obvious. If it's obvious at all," I said.

"Right. Then you will text us when it's clear, and we will make our way across the street," Mackenzie added.

"So," Larry said and started clapping his hands together, "sounds good."

"Yeah. We go to the door that you will leave unlocked. We have our pepper spray ready. We have pocketknives just in case. Go in and make things as quick as possible!" I said, sounding excited, which I did not expect.

"Then make our way back to the car and make our way back to the hotel," Mackenzie added, also sounding excited.

We thought it would be a good idea to reserve a hotel room instead of going back to our houses. I told my parents I would be staying at Mackenzie's place. Like usual, they got all strict and questioned me. They asked if her parents would be there and if I could call when I got there and call again before I went to bed. Before they said more, I cut them off, saying I was an adult and that I wouldn't be calling them once again. I just ran out of the house.

"I think going to a hotel is a pretty awesome idea," Larry said.

"So what do we do now?" I asked.

"I guess we hang out here for a while. Then change when it's time and make sure we have everything we need ready to go," Mackenzie said calmly, like what we were about to do was no big deal.

"Then it's all good," Larry said. "Well, I'm gonna head out, get food, and get ready for work."

"Just act natural," Mackenzie said.

"I'll be fine. That asshole deserves this!" Larry chuckled.

"We'll see you in the morning then," I said.

"See you ladies later," he replied. He got up, tapping the table with a smile on his face, and left us on our own.

"This is gonna be one hell of a night," I said more to myself than to Mackenzie.

"It sure is," she said, looking down.

"If you want to back out, now would be the time."

"No way! I'm not gonna leave you!"
"Thanks," I said.
"What are best friends for?"

CHAPTER 11

IT WAS 9:45 P.M. IT was dark and raining. I just knew that we would track up the floor like crazy when we went into Speedway. I could just imagine water and possibly mud being all over the floor. We were bound to leave footprints behind. I was planning on throwing my shoes away after this anyways, so hopefully, there wouldn't be any problems there.

We were both dressed in solid black. I was even wearing black socks just to be extra safe. We had driven to the closest Dick's Sporting Goods to buy our solid black ski masks. I had mine sitting on my lap, ready to go.

"This shirt is all itchy," Mackenzie complained from the passenger seat. "I'm not used to wearing long sleeves."

"It's just this one time. I'm sure you can manage," I said.

"Sure. If you say so. What time is it?"

"It's now nine fifty-one. I don't know if I can do this." I was gripping the steering wheel so tight that my skin was turning pink.

"Do not say that now! I'm here with you! Even though I can't believe it, but I'm going to see this through just like Larry," Mackenzie shot back. "Plus, you said you were in. That you wanted to do something crazy, remember?"

"You're right," I said, taking a deep breath and releasing my grip on the steering wheel.

"Damn straight, I'm right."

I looked over at her then. In all black. Black shoes, her black gloves, her black ski mask on her lap. I've never seen her dressed this way before.

"We can do this. I mean, if it's just Larry's boss, we can handle just one person. Two of us, one of him," I said, trying to relax myself.

"There you go. Now you're thinking," she said, pumping her fist. She gave me a quick fist bump. That actually made me smile.

"So we do this, then come back to the car, Larry's car, and go to the hotel, right?" I asked.

"Yup."

"It all just sounds so simple," I said.

"It does, but it's not," she replied, looking at me with a smug look on her face. I couldn't help but laugh.

"Larry might be right. This could be a thrill," I said.

"That's what I'm thinking," she replied. One more look at the car clock told me we had three minutes before Larry got off. Three minutes before I was about to commit my first crime.

"So time to finish the last touches," I said, nervously looking at Mackenzie.

"Right."

We both pulled our hair back, making sure it stayed under the ski masks. I also made sure my shoelaces were nice and tight. Just to be safe. Mackenzie reached into the back seat to grab the bag for the money. It was just a carry-on bag, but it should do the trick.

Just then I got a text. Larry just said he got off.

"It's showtime."

CHAPTER 12

MACKENZIE AND I WATCHED FROM across the street as Larry stepped outside and walked around the corner. He usually parked around the corner, so he walked around the corner again tonight to make things seem normal. Not that anyone would notice. That's when we made our move.

We got out of Larry's car, slipping on our ski masks at the same time. We quickly looked for traffic before crossing the street. All clear. We actually ran across the street. It was just pouring out now; it felt like my jeans were already sticking to me, but I kept moving. When we reached the door, we looked at each other, nodded, and then ran inside! I just made it a few feet inside before I choked! What I saw scared the living hell out of me! What I saw was a very intimidating man!

Chuck had to have been at least six feet tall, maybe taller! He looked like he was 350 pounds! I couldn't tell if it was muscle or fat! This would have been a piece of information I would love to have known about. I had two thoughts running through my mind just then. First, how in the hell are we supposed to rob this guy with only pepper spray? Second, if we pull this off, I'm going to kill Larry for not telling me about the size of this guy!

Mackenzie didn't seem intimidated by him. She grabbed my arm and pulled me along. She seemed to take total control. She quickly grabbed her pepper spray out of her pocket. I followed suit.

"Hey, you!" she shouted at Chuck. He looked up from the register. He already had cash in his hands and was counting it.

"What do you think you two are doing?" he demanded.

"We're taking all the money in the register and safe!" Mackenzie shouted.

Chuck just started laughing. He was laughing so hard that he dropped the money back in the register and grabbed his stomach.

"Oh, this is too good!" he said while trying to pull himself together. "So tell me, who put you up to this, huh?"

"Nobody! This is a real robbery! So hand over the money now!" I shouted, holding up my pepper spray, feeling like a damn fool.

"Really, sweetie? No guns? I would think every robbery would require guns," Chuck said, laughing again.

"Not always!" Mackenzie shouted with lots of attitude in her voice. She ran up to Chuck as he was looking at the floor, laughing. He looked up then, looking almost scared. They made direct eye contact for just a few seconds before she shot him directly in the eyes with the pepper spray!

"You fucking bitch!" he shouted as he grabbed his eyes. He was cursing so much and was shouting so loud that I thought someone would hear him and come racing in at any moment!

"Hurry!" Mackenzie shouted. She opened the carry-on bag and stepped over Chuck as he lay on the floor, screaming in pain. He fell to the floor because he couldn't see at the moment, had tripped over his own feet, and fell to the floor.

She was quickly grabbing all the money from the register as I was making my way around the screaming Chuck and going to the safe under the register. I took one look at Chuck and could see how the skin around his eyes was all red and irritated. I honestly felt bad, but it was too late now. I'm sure if Larry saw Chuck like this, he may say he deserved that too.

"So do we take the coins too or just the cash?" Mackenzie asked.

"Screw the coins, just the cash!" I said, a bit irritated.

"Got it."

I took every bit of cash from the safe and tossed it into the bag with the cash from the register. It looked to be a very large amount of money by the looks of it. Score!

"You bitches!" Chuck screamed from the floor. "You will never get away with this! You hear me?"

"We already have," Mackenzie replied while zipping up the bag. She then stepped over Chuck once again and started heading back to the door while I just stood there. I was looking at something I just had to get, mainly because it was something I had never tried before.

"Hey, get back here!" I shouted. Mackenzie spun around. I could tell by just looking at her eyes that she was saying, "We need to hurry the hell up."

"What now?" she asked, sounding paranoid now. Who could blame her?

"I gotta get these," I said, pointing toward the counter.

"Scratch-offs? You gotta be kidding!"

"Just open the damn bag!"

She did, and I started looking at the tickets, knowing damn well we had to move our asses.

"I'm gonna get two high rollers, holy shit! Fifty dollars each! Well, they're free right now!" I said, laughing. Even though it was kind of muffled through the ski mask, Mackenzie tried to laugh too, but she just sounded way too nervous.

This entire time, Chuck was still on the floor. He wasn't screaming or cursing as much now, but he still couldn't see much yet. I guess I was taking full advantage of that right now.

"I'll get four of the cash attack, four of the lucky lakes. Oh, this looks cute. I'll get five of the honey money," I continued.

"Girl, you really need to hurry up! The longer we're in here, the worse it gets!" She was starting to freak out now. I was nervous and scared too. I was just trying to make the best out of the situation.

"You do realize that it's still pouring out, right?" I asked. I was trying to calm us both down at that point.

"Okay, I get it. It may not be clear enough for someone to see us. Just grab your damn scratch-off, and let's go!"

"Almost done," I replied.

"Oh my god!" she replied, throwing her head back.

"So I'll get four of the sevens, four of the I'm to summer, six of the money trees, and that should do it," I said, throwing all the scratch-offs into the bag Mackenzie was holding open for me.

As I was walking over Chuck again and back around the counter, I felt a hand grab my ankle.

"You're not going anywhere, little girl!" Chuck shouted. "You hear me?"

I looked at him. His eyes were open and bloodshot. The skin around his eyes looked horrible. It almost looked like his eyes were bleeding.

He pulled my ankle, causing me to fall against the counter. I caught myself just in time.

"I need some help!" I yelled to Mackenzie.

"Holy shit!" She dropped the bag, came by the counter, and saw that Chuck had a hold of my ankle.

"Hold on, I'll be right back!" She then ran toward the pop.

"Really? Where are you going?" She didn't answer.

"I may not be able to see real well, but I believe your friend just ditched you." Chuck chuckled. Just hearing him chuckle sent a shiver down my spine.

"No, she didn't. She wouldn't leave me!" I shouted at Chuck.

"Whatever you say."

Right then, I kicked Chuck right in the face with my free foot. My heel hit his jaw, but his grip on my ankle didn't ease up.

"Fuck!" he shouted. "You two will regret this! I promise you!"

"I don't think so," Mackenzie said, returning with a twelve-pack of Mountain Dew.

She had it raised above her head and was charging at Chuck. She brought the pop down hard right on Chuck's back, then again and again. By the fourth hit, Chuck finally released his grip on my ankle. I took off for the door. I looked back, and Mackenzie was still beating Chuck with the pop! It was kind of funny actually. I was looking at an eighteen-year-old girl dressed in all black, beating a large man with a twelve-pack of Mountain Dew. Good times. I couldn't help but laugh a little bit. I'm sure Chuck was in pain, but shit happens.

"Are you done yet? Or are you having too much fun?" Now it was my turn to laugh. Chuck was once again cursing and in more pain.

"Oh, I kinda got carried away," she said, laughing too.

"That shit isn't funny! You're gonna regret all this!" Chuck shouted, now holding his back in pain.

"Huh-uh, whatever you say." Mackenzie grabbed the bag and started heading for the door. Then she stopped. She headed back toward the register, grabbed a bunch of candy, tossed it in the bag, and then looked at me.

"Really?" I asked.

"Really." She chuckled.

Then we finally ran back out the door and back out into the pouring rain.

CHAPTER 13

IT WAS ABOUT 11:30 P.M. before Officers Derek Clarkson and Emily Lynn arrived at Speedway. The rain had become a light sprinkle by that point, but the wet tracks of the two suspects were still very clear on the floor. They did their best to walk around them.

"Excuse me, is anyone here?" Officer Clarkson asked.

"I'm here," Chuck answered. He was walking out of the bathroom. His eyes were still bloodshot, and his skin looked terrible.

"Sir, are you all right?" Officer Lynn asked, concerned.

"Hell, no, I ain't all right. I had a couple of kids rob me! One bitch sprayed me with pepper spray!" He pointed at his eyes.

"Are you Chuck Wilson? The man who called about a robbery?" Officer Lynn asked.

"Are you a damn rookie? Isn't it obvious?" Chuck shouted. "Hell yeah, it was me! I was just in the bathroom, trying to clean this crap out of my eyes."

"Just settle down, sir," Officer Clarkson began, "Just start from the top, and we can help you."

"Son of a bitch." Chuck rolled his eyes; he had his hands on his hips.

"Mr. Wilson, the more details you can give us, the more we can help you," Officer Clarkson said, bringing out a notepad and a pen.

So Chuck told the officers everything that happened. Even the humiliating parts, like having a young small girl spray him with pepper spray and then having that same girl beat him with Mountain Dew. Officer Clarkson was taking notes and tried his best not to laugh when Chuck talked about getting hit with pop.

"Are you laughing at me?"

"No, sir. I was trying not to sneeze," he lied.

"Look, I only know so much because I was blind most of the time," Chuck said.

"So what you're saying is that you heard most of it, right?" Officer Lynn asked, raising her eyebrows.

"Yeah, I guess. I felt it too though! My eyes and skin burning and pain from getting hit with my own damn pop!"

"Can you describe the suspects for us? Height, weight, hair color, anything at all?" Officer Clarkson asked.

"Not really, honestly. Two white females. One was about 5" 8', the other maybe 5" 5'. I knew they were white because I could see some skin around their eyes. They were dressed in all black. Even black gloves and black ski masks. They must have had their hair pulled back or something because I didn't see any hair," Chuck said. He was starting to calm down.

"They were small girls, real skinny," he continued. "They both had to be under 200 pounds."

"Was there anything else?" Officer Lynn asked. She seemed to be very interested in Chuck's story.

"Nope. That about sums it up."

"Okay. Well, here's my card. If you can think of anything else, call me," she said, handing him a card.

"Same here. Here's my card also." Officer Clarkson followed suit, handing Chuck his card.

"Will do, Officers," Chuck replied, giving them a half-ass sarcastic salute.

"We'll get back to you if we know anything. In the meantime, get some rest," Officer Lynn said.

"Yup" was all Chuck said.

"Good night, Mr. Wilson," Officer Clarkson said, shaking Chuck's hand.

"Good night, Officers."

They headed back toward their car. Once inside, they sat quietly for a few minutes.

"I don't know why, but something seemed odd about that," Officer Lynn said. "We have very little to go on."

"I think so too. It also feels that we can't do much here," Officer Clarkson responded.

"Right," Officer Lynn sighed.

"Let's call it a night."

Officer Clarkson started the car, and they drove off into the rainy night.

CHAPTER 14

"RACHAEL! RACHAEL! WAKE UP!" MACKENZIE shouted from the bed next to mine. "Your damn phone keeps going off."

After the robbery, we jumped into Larry's car and drove around for a while before coming to Motel 6. We wanted to make sure we weren't being followed. It seemed clear.

"Shit!" I rolled over and grabbed my phone, seeing seven missed calls from my parents. I also noticed the time.

"There's no way that it's almost noon!" I was shocked.

"Are you serious?" Mackenzie grabbed her phone. "Holy shit!"

"I got seven missed calls from my parents! I should say holy shit to that!"

"What are you going to tell them?"

"I have no idea."

"You did say you would be staying at my place, right?" she asked.

"Yeah, but seven missed calls is a bit much," I said. "I gotta call them back."

"You do that," Mackenzie said.

I called home first, and my dad answered on the second ring.

"Rachael, where have you been? Your mom and I have been worried!" He actually sounded paranoid.

"I'm at Mackenzie's, remember, Dad? There's nothing to worry about!"

"You just haven't missed calls from us. What have you been up to?"

I had to come up with a lie very fast. I already felt horrible about lying in general, but I never had to come up with a lie on the spot.

31

"We went to a movie. Then went back to her place to binge-watch our favorite TV show." I hoped this new lie would work. "Our phones were on silent the entire time. I'm sorry for not checking it sooner."

"Okay, if you say so," my dad replied, not sounding totally convinced.

"Have I ever given you or Mom any reason to doubt me?" I asked.

"No. None at all. Just keep in touch, okay?"

"Okay, fine!" I answered. I just hung up the phone and tossed it on the bed.

"They're being paranoid and controlling again, huh?" Mackenzie asked.

"Yup." I fell back on the pillow with my hands covering my face for a couple of minutes.

"I never lied before. I feel so guilty. I feel like total crap actually," I said, almost crying.

"I can understand that. It's gonna be hard to break free and do your own thing," she said, trying to be comforting.

"Speaking of that, we still didn't count what we got from last night!" I said, starting to jump out of bed. Just then we heard a loud pounding on the door. Mackenzie and I looked at each other with huge eyes! We just froze in place.

"Police! Open up!"

CHAPTER 15

"WHAT THE FUCK!" MACKENZIE LIPPED the words to me very slowly. We both knew there was no way anybody suspected us or even knew where we were. After we drove off, we pulled over by a dark wooded area and changed our clothes. All our black clothing had been put into a large black bag, tied tight, and thrown into a dumpster.

"Police! Open up! Don't make me break down this door!"

"Wait a minute! I know that voice!" I jumped off my bed and ran to the door. I looked through the peephole.

"I'm going to kill this bastard!" I said to Mackenzie. I was relieved and mad at the same time.

"Who is it?" Mackenzie asked, still wide-eyed.

I opened the door and stood aside to allow Larry to walk in! As he walked in, he was laughing!

"You asshole!" Mackenzie shouted, throwing a pillow at him. "You scared the hell out of us!"

"Maybe that was the idea!" Larry said, laughing again.

"You suck!" Mackenzie said, now folding her arms.

All Larry could do was continue to laugh.

"You wanna hear something really funny?" I asked.

"What's that?" Larry stopped laughing and looked at me.

"Somebody failed to mention the size of their boss!"

Larry's expression quickly changed. He suddenly looked serious; he looked very attractive that way too.

I just stood there with my arms crossed, trying to give him the type of look that said, "I'm about to kick your butt!"

33

"Okay, I get it. If I told you how big Chuck was, you two would have never pulled that! You both would have backed out!"

"Are you serious? You should have mentioned that no matter what!" I said, pushing him. I also smacked him across the head.

"What was that for?"

"You had that coming," Mackenzie said, finally getting out of bed.

"So wanna see what we got, Rachael?" she asked.

"For sure."

I went to the bathroom, to the tub where we tossed the bag when we first went to the motel. There really weren't many hiding places, so we just tossed the bag in the tub for safekeeping.

"Really? The tub?" Larry asked sarcastically.

"Shut up before I smack you again," I replied. Larry just put his hands in the air and pressed his lips together.

I dropped the bag on my bed, slowly unzipping it. I couldn't believe we had just robbed someone the night before, and now here I was about to count what Mackenzie and I stole.

"I can't hold back on this one," Larry said, starting to laugh again as he was looking over my shoulder and into the bag. "You also stole scratch-offs and candy! I love it!"

"Hey, just for the record, Rachael wanted the scratch-offs, and I thought we might get hungry," Mackenzie said, looking at me. Just then we both started to laugh.

"Let's count this. We can't just leave this out in the open!" I said.

"Let's do it," Mackenzie said, rubbing her hands together. She took half the cash out, carried it over to her bed, and started counting. I took out the scratch-offs and handed all but one to Larry.

"Would you like something fun to do?" I asked.

"Sure. Why not." He smiled. He sat down at the end of my bed, took out a coin, and went at it. I took out the rest of the cash and started counting it.

The room was very quiet for a while while we were all counting. I actually got hungry, reached into the bag, and grabbed some M&M's. Just the noise of the bag sounded really loud in a quiet room. Larry and Mackenzie both looked at me and started laughing.

"Shut up!" I said, laughing.

"Well, you did good on these tickets. There's $250 here. That's nice," Larry said.

"Way to go, Rachael. You stole some winners," Mackenzie joked.

The room got quiet again as Larry waited patiently for us to finish counting the money.

"I'm done," Mackenzie said, tossing the money back into the bag.

"Same. What do you have?" She had been using her calculator on her phone. I was doing the same. I added my total to hers and was shocked.

"Holy shit! We got $2,418! That's a good business day for a Monday at Speedway!" I said, shocked.

Larry just whistled.

"Damn!" Mackenzie was once again wide-eyed. "So what now?" she asked.

"No clue. I guess we split it. Larry, do you want anything for helping us out?" I asked.

"Nope. I'm good honestly. I just love how Chuck got what he finally deserved," Larry said.

"Are you positive?" Mackenzie asked.

"Yup," he replied.

"Just keep the winnings from the scratch-offs," I said.

"That's fair. Works for me," he replied. "Was that ticket you got a winner?"

"Let me check." Just then Larry got a phone call. He seemed real jittery. This time, he got wide-eyed as he looked at the two of us.

Larry hung up the phone and held it tight in his hands.

"What?" Mackenzie and I asked in unison.

"Two officers questioned Chuck last night. He didn't know much though," Larry said.

"How could you know that?" Mackenzie asked.

"One of the officers who questioned him was Officer Emily Lynn," he said.

"And…" I said.

"Officer Emily Lynn is my mom."

CHAPTER 16

"ARE YOU SERIOUS RIGHT NOW?" I shouted. "I know we haven't been friends for long, but how could you not mention that your mom is a cop?"

"We are totally screwed!" Mackenzie shouted, falling back onto the bed and screaming into a pillow.

"It's gonna be okay," Larry said calmly. "My mom won't suspect a thing."

"How can you be so sure?" I asked.

"Just try to calm down. Take a deep breath."

"How am I supposed to calm down, huh? I don't wanna go to jail!"

"That won't happen." Larry gently grabbed my shoulders. It felt good actually. "My mom knows that I work at a Speedway, but she doesn't know which one."

"How is that comforting?" Mackenzie shouted. She got off the bed, now smacking Larry in the head.

"Okay, I deserved that. You two just need to breathe and try to calm down."

"How do we do that exactly?" Mackenzie shouted.

"First of all, you both should stop shouting before someone hears you!"

Mackenzie and I just looked at each other and took a deep breath, and we both sat down on my bed.

"Okay, you got a good point," I said, releasing a deep breath.

Larry sat down on Mackenzie's bed across from us. He placed his hands on his knees.

"So my mom and I are not very close. It sucks. I didn't mention it before because it's a touchy subject and something I don't like to talk about," Larry explained. "My parents got a divorce about five years ago. It was rough. My mom wasn't around much because of her job. My dad literally gave her an option. Her job or us. You can guess which one she chose." Larry looked like he was about to choke up. I really wasn't sure what to do.

"I know I mentioned earlier that I was trying to prove to both my parents that I can hold a job, but it's really just my dad," Larry continued.

"I didn't know that," I said softly.

"It's okay. Maybe helping you two out with this was me acting out in multiple ways," he said.

"Are you sure she won't suspect anything?" Mackenzie whispered.

"Yeah. She called me just now for the first time in a long time just to tell me to be careful. She told me about a robbery at a Speedway last night. That they don't have much to go on either."

"That's comforting. Chuck only got to see our eyes," I said. "I'm not too worried though."

"Just act natural around everyone, and you two should be all right," Larry said. He sounded very confident.

"Right." Mackenzie rolled her eyes. "Did Chuck give a description of who robbed him?"

"I don't know," Larry said. "But no worries, just relax, and it will all be okay."

"How? We still need to stash the money somewhere!" I said with some attitude.

"Oh shit! I almost forgot about that!" Mackenzie said, falling back on the bed.

"I may be able to help you with that," Larry replied. "My house has a small attic, and the entrance is in my closet. If you want, I can keep it there," he suggested. I had to admit to myself that I at least thought it was a good idea.

"Then if you guys want any of the cash, you can just let me know."

"Sounds good to me," Mackenzie said, sitting up again.

"Same here," I replied. "But wouldn't it look suspicious?"

"You guys put it all into a carry-on bag. It just looks like luggage. There's nothing suspicious about that." Larry chuckled.

"We can't think straight right now," Mackenzie said. "We got a lot going on." That made all of us laugh.

"At least let us take the candy out before you take it."

CHAPTER 17

"I DON'T KNOW HOW I feel about this. You haven't been home for the past three days," my dad said, sounding concerned. This was going to be a fun phone call.

"Once again, I'm eighteen now. I'm considered an adult. But I feel like a baby when I'm always checking in with you and Mom," I replied.

Mackenzie and I were still at the Motel 6. We didn't quite feel like we could act natural around everybody quite yet. We needed more time.

"I know you're eighteen, Rachael. I don't need the constant reminder," he said with a deep tone in his voice now. "You may think your mom and I are too strict, but we want you to stay out of trouble."

Too late for that, I thought.

"I get it. I just needed to get out of the house."

"Just keep that attitude under control and come home soon!"

"Oh my god! I hardly have an attitude, and I feel like staying away longer when you guys try to control me!" I was almost shouting.

"You just won't understand until you have kids," he replied.

I could just roll my eyes back and do a deep sigh.

"And answer your phone when we call. Can you do that?" he asked.

"Okay fine. Can I go now?" I asked, irritated.

"Fine. I'll talk to you later. Be careful."

"Bye."

I hung up my phone and, this time, tossed it on the floor.

"Your dad doesn't sound too happy," Mackenzie said while brushing her teeth.

"Nope. He says to come home soon and says I have an attitude."

"Parents, right?" Mackenzie replied and then spit into the sink.

"Yup," I said with my hands over my eyes. "So when will Larry get here?" I asked.

We knew that if we stayed at the motel longer, we needed things. Mackenzie and I wanted to stay at the motel instead of getting things for ourselves. Larry seemed to understand.

"He should be here soon. He says he needs to make it quick though because he needs to work."

"That's cool."

Mackenzie had been the one paying for the motel stay this entire time but didn't seem to mind.

"Do you want me to pay you for half of the motel stay?" I asked.

She had been saving up money from tutoring her neighbor, who was in middle school.

"No, it's fine. It's kind of an exciting way to spend money!" She laughed. "Plus, I got the money back from Speedway!"

"That's a good point." We both had to chuckle at that.

"We gotta remember to ask Larry about any updates on that," I said.

"That just makes me nervous," she said, standing by my bed. "I mean, we haven't seen anything on the news about it, so that's a good thing, right?" she asked.

"I can only hope so."

Right then, there was a knock on the door. Mackenzie went to answer it. Larry was here with our supplies.

"Hey, girls! How's it hanging?"

"You really wanna know? It's getting kind of boring," Mackenzie replied, closing the door.

"I can imagine. Get out and get some fresh air. That should help," he said, setting down the bags with our things in them.

"I'm just curious about one thing," I said.

"If you're about to ask about any updates, then I gotta tell you there's nothing. Chuck didn't have much to go on, so what he told my mom and her partner turned into a dead end." He grinned. "Looks as if you two got away with it!"

"Are you really serious?" Mackenzie asked, incredibly shocked and wide-eyed. "They have no leads, no anything?"

"Nope. Not from what I understand," Larry replied.

Mackenzie was so happy and relieved that she started jumping up and down and making some sort of shrieking noise. Larry was just watching her with a large grin on his face. I was sitting on my bed with my legs crossed, but I somehow managed to keep my cool. A huge weight did fall off my shoulders, and I was able to relax, but now I was only thinking one thing.

What's next?

CHAPTER 18

OFFICER EMILY LYNN WAS SITTING at her desk, staring at her computer screen. She had a cup of coffee to the right of her keyboard and a stack of paperwork to the left. It was ten on a Monday morning. It had been a week since the Speedway robbery, but something was still eating at her nerves. She just knew there had to be more to it, like how did the suspects get in when it was closed and the doors should have been locked?

"You all right there, partner?" Derek asked from his desk, which was to the right of hers. "You look like you're staring off into space." Emily jumped a little bit.

"Oh sorry. I was just thinking about the Speedway robbery."

"Really? What about it? I know it's only been a week, but what we got from Chuck was vague."

"I know, but something isn't right," she replied.

"Like what?" Derek asked.

"I know what Chuck told us was weak and that he didn't call us with more information, but he never mentioned why the door was unlocked," she said, rubbing her temples.

"Well, maybe the employee who left for the night forgot to lock it," Derek started but realized something. "Hold it! There should have been two people there! Chuck shouldn't have been alone!" Derek was wide-eyed and seemed to have surprised himself.

"Exactly," Emily said, looking Derek in the eyes. "There had to have been a third person involved."

"I should have caught that before. I feel like a damn idiot," Derek said, falling back into his chair.

"It's not your fault. Chuck didn't mention it," Emily replied. "Hey, Derek, can I trust you with something?" Emily asked in a half-whisper.

"Really? You know damn well you can!" Derek whispered back. "You can tell me anything."

"Okay," she sighed. "My son works at a Speedway."

CHAPTER 19

"ARE YOU SERIOUS?" DEREK ASKED, practically shouting now and getting the attention of others.

"Calm down! Really?" Emily put a finger to her lips that said, "Sssshhhh."

"Sorry, everyone." Derek directed his attention to everyone who heard him. "My mistake."

"Why didn't you mention this before?" he asked.

"I just wasn't sure. My son and I are pretty distant. I don't know if he would ever be involved in something like this."

"Um, okay. It sounds like you may be giving him the benefit of the doubt here, but okay," Derek replied.

"Thanks," she said annoyed. "But it's my fault we're distant."

"If you're referring to your divorce, then I get it. I remember that. It was a tough time."

"Me being more involved with my job than my family led to that. The divorce was my fault. It's also my fault that I've been so distant from my own son," Emily said, almost in tears.

"You can't be so tough on yourself," Derek said, not knowing what to say.

Emily looked up at Derek from her desk. He was standing next to her now with his arms crossed. She could tell he was trying to be comforting but didn't know how.

"I will always blame myself no matter what anybody else says. It's unforgivable. I neglected my own son. I only know where he works. I don't know if he would act out," she replied. She put her head in her hands, still holding back tears.

Derek placed a hand on Emily's shoulder, still not knowing how to comfort her.

"If there's anything you need, just let me know," he said in a soft tone.

"Actually, there is," she said, raising her head and looking him straight in the eyes. "I need you to help me figure out exactly which Speedway my son works at."

CHAPTER 20

I WAS FINALLY BACK AT home after what seemed like forever. I was lying on my own bed now, stretched out and relaxed. I actually missed everything about it. I missed my pillows, my blankets, and most of all, I missed the posters I had on my ceiling. The ones I was looking at now. One was of the grumpy cat saying I hate vacation; one was of Michael Jackson in his Billie Jean outfit, and the third was of my favorite TV show, *Supernatural*.

My parents had questioned my whereabouts. It wasn't surprising. I wanted to scream at them, but I also understood their concern. It was almost a two-hour conversation. I told them I was at Mackenzie's because I just needed a break. They didn't accept that answer. I finally said I needed time away from them and their strict ways. That didn't go over so well. My mom said that if I didn't change my attitude, she would send me to therapy. That's a bit over the top. My dad sort of agreed, but not fully. He said my attitude wasn't that bad but that it was headed in that direction. Once again, I was asking, "What attitude?" Maybe I had an attitude, but nowhere near enough to be sent to therapy!

Anyway, long story short, I stopped paying attention to them. I was just standing there in our kitchen, pretending to listen while they went on and on about who knows what. I finally snuck out and found my way to my bedroom.

So now I'm just staring up at my ceiling, looking from one poster to another, just trying to relax. Mackenzie's parents are not like this. She told them she was staying with me, and that was that. No questions asked. Lucky.

I jumped when my cell phone started to ring. It was Larry.

"Hey, what's up?" I asked.

"Hey! Just wondering if you would want to meet a friend of mine. He's a pretty cool guy!" Larry sounded pretty excited about it too.

"Um, that seems kind of random."

"Maybe. Maybe not. He's also a coworker. He knows what happened to Chuck, and he absolutely loved it!"

"What?" I shouted, now bolting up in bed. "Did you tell people about what we did?" I was starting to panic a little bit.

"Oh, no, no, no! Chuck told someone when that person asked about his eyes! That person spread the story along! It's all good though!" Larry responded.

"So your coworker told you about it?" I asked.

"Yup. I laughed again, just picturing it again. I bet it was pretty hilarious!" Larry started to laugh.

"I bet if it was on camera, you would watch it over and over again." That's when it hit me. Cameras! Speedway had to have cameras!

"Oh fuck!" I shouted into Larry's ear, not realizing it.

"Ouch! What was that?" he asked.

"Speedway has cameras, right?" I asked in a panic again.

"I think so. Why?" Larry asked. There was a short pause, and before I could answer, he responded, "Oh fuck!"

CHAPTER 21

"I CAN'T BELIEVE WE MISSED something!" Emily shouted. "We are both slacking!"

"Officer Lynn, can you please keep it down? I'm trying to fill out a report here!" another officer said to Emily as she walked by.

"I'm so sorry, Officer Brooks. It won't happen again!"

Derek was sitting by his desk, just finishing up a phone call. He held up a finger to Emily, saying just a minute. Emily took a seat in a chair next to his desk. She was so antsy she couldn't sit still.

"Okay, talk to you later," Derek said, hanging up the phone. Then he directed all his attention to his partner.

"So what did we miss? Why are you so anxious?" he asked, very confused.

"The cameras! We forgot about the cameras!" Emily said, hitting her own leg.

"What are you talking about?"

"Really? Speedway! We didn't bother to ask about the cameras!"

"Are you serious? We did forget, didn't we?" Derek closed his eyes and let his head fall backward. "How is that even possible?" he asked.

"I was thinking about that. I think we forgot because the story Chuck told us was just too hilarious. Maybe we got thrown off by that," Emily said, tapping her index finger on the desk now.

"It was one of the funnier stories I heard, I'll admit that." He chuckled. "But that's still not a good enough excuse."

"Either way, we need to go back to Speedway," Emily replied.

"We may need to get a search warrant first. Don't jump too far ahead," Derek said, sitting straight.

"Well, maybe not. There's no solid case or evidence really. We really need to see the surveillance once, and that should be enough," Emily said, now standing up.

"Maybe. You could be right." Emily could tell Derek was starting to hesitate. She had seen this before.

"Look. We just need to go now! This has really been bothering me, and I just need to see it, okay?" Emily had started to shout again.

"Ssshhhh." Derek put his finger to his mouth. "I can clearly see that you're anxious, and I know that it's bothering you, but right now, you need to relax. Can you do that?"

Emily looked down at him. Her look was saying, "Are you serious?" but also saying, "You're right." She slowly lowered herself back into the chair and crossed her arms.

"I can't make any promises, but I can try."

"Okay. I can work with that," Derek said with a smile. "Let's do it then. Let's make another trip to Speedway."

"Thank you," Emily said with relief. "You're the best!"

"When do we leave?"

"As soon as possible."

CHAPTER 22

"NO, NO, NO! WE WERE supposed to be in the clear, but now we could be screwed!" Mackenzie shouted.

After I hung up with Larry, I called Mackenzie and told her about the cameras. We were at the park near my place now.

"Oh my god, I know. Tell me about it." I had time to calm down on my walk to the park, but I was still scared.

"So where's Larry? Why isn't he here?"

"He had to go to work. He was asked to cover a shift."

"Can he keep his cool at work?" Mackenzie asked, worried. I couldn't help but laugh just then.

"Huh, hello? What's so funny? There's nothing funny about this!" Mackenzie was irritated now.

"Sorry, you just asked that after Larry worked that day, knowing Chuck would be robbed. He kept his cool then, so I'm not worried now."

"Oh duh!" She playfully slapped her head. "I knew that."

We were both sitting down at a bench now, laughing. It felt good to laugh, especially at a time like this.

"So Larry was also wondering if I wanted to meet a friend of his. He's also a coworker. I never answered him yet," I said casually.

"Do you know much about him?" Mackenzie asked, curious.

"Nope. We didn't get that far. He loves what you and I did to Chuck. I know that much." I smiled.

"I have to admit that was kinda fun." She smiled. "But we also need to focus on the cameras now."

"Right. Well, Chuck couldn't give the police a good description of us, so maybe the cameras didn't catch much either," I said, trying to stay positive.

"Okay, I can buy that. Way to think positive. So what about the police?" she asked.

"What about them?"

"They have to know they missed that by now. If not, they suck."

"Maybe," I replied. I was thinking about something now.

"What are you thinking about?"

"Well, it's been ten days now since we did what we did, you know, the big showdown, and you would have thought someone would have checked the cameras. Larry would have told us," I replied, but I was also half thinking to myself.

"I forgot all about that code name!" Mackenzie shook her head and smiled. "Well, maybe someone did check the cameras when Larry wasn't working," she suggested.

"That's true." I was still scared about it though. Anything could happen. Just then something did happen.

I jumped when my phone vibrated in my back pocket. It said it was a text from Larry, but the text itself wasn't Larry.

"Can this get any worse?" I asked, almost freaking out now.

"What is it?" Mackenzie asked, wide-eyed and nervous.

"It's a text from Larry's phone, but Larry didn't send it," I said, still looking at my phone.

"What does it say?"

"It says, 'Hey, this is Larry's friend JoJo from work. He gave me his phone to tell you that the police are here! They are asking to see the camera footage!'"

CHAPTER 23

LARRY WAS AT WORK AT one of the registers. He had been asked to help JoJo because it had gotten busy fast, but just one look outside the window had made him freeze in place.

"Dude, people need help, move it!" JoJo had said impatiently when he had noticed that Larry was just standing there.

JoJo was a friend Larry had just recently met at work. He honestly hadn't meant to make friends at work but had made an exception for JoJo. JoJo was Hispanic and just very funny but very focused and dedicated to his work when he had to be. It was now that he was impatient with Larry for just standing there, looking out the window!

"Hello? Can you hear me?" JoJo yelled.

Larry seemed to be in some sort of trance, and when he slowly turned back around to help a customer, JoJo just knew something was wrong.

"Dude, what's wrong?" JoJo asked, concerned.

"The police are here," Larry said in a whisper that JoJo could hardly make out.

JoJo's eyes got big. He did his best to focus on helping the customers. He knew they had come back to talk about the robbery. By now, every employee knew about it.

Larry couldn't stay at the register. He saw the two officers get out of the car and are now approaching the door. He recognized his mom instantly!

"Holy fuck." Larry grabbed his phone quickly and handed it to JoJo. "Here take this. Text Rachael. Look under contacts. You'll find her number. I'll explain later." Then Larry took off.

"What the hell, man?" JoJo shouted, but Larry was already gone. JoJo was left with a line of customers and questions he had no answers to.

Larry had run to hide in the back of the store. He didn't want his mom to see him. He was hoping that JoJo wouldn't slip up and mention his name to the police. But JoJo didn't know better. He had no idea who his mom was.

Another employee had come up to help on the registers now, the same time the police had just walked in. They spotted JoJo first.

"Hello. My name is Officer Lynn. This is my partner, Officer Clarkson. We're here to speak to Chuck Wilson. Is he around?" Emily asked JoJo.

"Um, I haven't seen him in a while," JoJo said nervously. "I've been busy helping customers."

"Do you know if he's in today?" Emily asked.

"Yeah, he's here somewhere," JoJo said.

"Is there any way you can let him know we're here?" she asked.

"Um, sure. I can look for him," JoJo replied, still nervous.

"You do that," Officer Lynn responded. JoJo quickly left the counter and headed in the same direction Larry had gone, but he didn't make it far.

"Why aren't you up at the register working?" Chuck asked in a pretty angry tone. JoJo almost ran into him as he was heading to the back.

"The police are here. They're looking for you," JoJo said, still nervous.

"What? Did they say why?" Chuck demanded.

"No, but they asked for you by name." JoJo seemed more confident now.

"It's gotta be about the most humiliating night of my life," Chuck said mostly to himself.

"I don't know."

"You get back to work. I'll go see what they want." Chuck just pushed JoJo off to the side and headed to the front of the store. JoJo followed out of curiosity.

"Hello again, Officers. What can I do for you?" Chuck asked when he saw them. He was putting up an act by acting nice. JoJo knew Chuck well enough to tell the difference.

"We're here about the robbery, Mr. Wilson," Officer Clark said. "We would like to take a look at your security surveillance if you don't mind."

"Why didn't you ask about that before? You two really are rookies, huh?" Chuck said with a smirk. Officer Clarkson seemed to let that comment slide.

"Can we take a look at it, please?"

"Well, yeah, that's what it's there for. Take it all. Do what you need to do," Chuck said with more of an attitude this time.

"Thank you."

Chuck led the officers away to a different part of the store. That's when JoJo remembered he had Larry's phone. He sent Rachael a text. Then he set off to find Larry.

CHAPTER 24

"DUDE. WHAT THE HELL IS going on?" JoJo asked, panicking. He had found Larry hiding in the back by the milk.

"It's a long story," Larry replied, sliding his hand through his hair. "It started out as one thing but became so much more."

"You better start explaining, dude."

"Not here. This is so not the place to talk about it," Larry said.

"Chuck took the officers to wherever the cameras were. They're still here," JoJo explained.

"Fuck!" Larry shouted, putting both hands on his head, "Shit."

"I feel like I'm part of something now. So can you tell me anything?" JoJo asked.

"Okay. I just need a minute." Larry took some deep breaths to try to pull himself together. It didn't quite help, but it was worth a shot.

"Did you see that female officer?" Larry asked, pointing toward the registers.

"Yeah. What about her?" JoJo seemed confused.

Larry looked straight into JoJo's eyes. He paused for a while before he answered. "You may not believe this, but she's my mom!"

"Are you serious? No way!" JoJo's eyes were huge now.

"I'm serious. There's one more thing," Larry said calmly now.

"Damn, man, what else?"

"Nobody knows this, but I played a part in the robbery."

CHAPTER 25

IT WAS THE NEXT AFTERNOON when Rachael, Larry, Mackenzie, and JoJo all met up at Subway. By now, Larry had told JoJo everything that happened from the very beginning—how Rachael wanted to do her own thing, how she had wanted to do something crazy, to how his mom, Officer Lynn, and her partner showed up at Speedway.

"Wow, guys. Just wow. I'm not sure what to say. Like I get wanting to do your own thing, but just wow," JoJo said in shock.

"So do you think we were totally crazy?" Rachael asked.

"Oh yeah, big time! But it's a good kind of crazy." JoJo chuckled. "I mean, it's a hell of a story. It kinda sounds like fun honestly."

"Really? You think so?" Mackenzie asked, kind of shocked.

"Yeah. It takes balls to do something like that. Like serious balls." He smiled.

"I just hope we don't get caught on camera," Mackenzie said, a little nervous.

"It was all my idea," Rachael said. "You guys didn't have to agree to anything."

"It was our decision," Larry replied. "It's our own fault if we get caught. So far, it's all good."

"He's right," Mackenzie agreed.

"Are you worried about the cameras?" Rachael asked, concerned.

"Not really," Mackenzie said with confidence. "We had our faces covered. They can't identify us. At least that's what I believe."

"That's a good point," Larry replied.

"Well, what about you? Was your face in view of the cameras when you left the door unlocked?" Rachael asked Larry. Larry now had a look of concern on his face.

"What's that look?" JoJo asked. "Did you now think about that?"

"Um, no, not really," Larry said. "I feel so stupid." He put his head down on the table and hit the table with his fist.

"What?" both Rachael and Mackenzie shouted in unison, both wide-eyed.

"Dude, you could be totally screwed!" JoJo exclaimed.

Larry looked up and made direct eye contact with him.

"No shit, man. Thanks for the reminder."

JoJo sat back in his seat, putting both hands in the air. "Sorry, bro."

"So don't be mad or anything, but what if your mom sees you on the footage?" Rachael asked in a soft tone. Larry's head was back on the table, and all he could manage was a soft moan.

"Well, if she does see him, I'm sure she will come back to the store. If she doesn't see him, then she may not come back, right?" JoJo asked, looking from one person to the other. Larry looked up at JoJo with a surprised look.

"You might be on to something. Maybe it could play out that way. Or maybe I could just lie," Larry said.

"Wait? What? She could always call you too, you know," Mackenzie said.

"True. Even if she did, I could lie like I said," Larry started. "I could say it was an accident."

"I don't know. Couldn't it make things worse between you guys?" Rachael asked, looking confused but also feeling that all this was her fault.

"We're already pretty distant, so don't worry about that. I don't see us getting closer any time soon. One little lie won't hurt," Larry said, starting to relax but just a little.

"Dude, just take it one step at a time. We don't know if the police have seen the footage yet. So we don't know if they saw you. So just for now, let's just relax," JoJo said calmly.

"That's easier said than done. You're right though. One step at a time," Larry responded, releasing a deep breath.

"So what now?" Mackenzie asked. "Do we just wait around to see what happens next?"

"Pretty much," Larry said. "We can't do anything else."

CHAPTER 26

OFFICER EMILY LYNN WAS JUST too eager to get everything all set up so she could see the surveillance footage. She was like a little girl in a candy shop.

"Is it ready yet? We could get some answers from this," she asked impatiently.

"It's close. Just give me a minute," Derek replied with a smirk. He knew how eager she was. He was trying to joke around with her.

"It's not close enough. I know before that I said something felt odd. Now I get to find out what that something is," she replied.

"That's right. You did say that. Let's just pay very close attention to every little detail." The tech was just finishing up everything the officers needed to play back the footage. The tech did this so much that it felt like another daily part of her regular routine. She still didn't know if that was a good or bad thing. Her name was Marie Phillips. She had been a tech for five years now and really seemed to enjoy it. Her favorite part was watching how eager people got before they saw the footage, like now. She was occasionally looking at Officer Lynn and smiling. It took all she had not to laugh. She had to remain professional.

"Okay, that outa do it. The monitor is a little dusty. I'll just clean that off for you," Marie said, smiling at Officer Lynn. Marie was just about to grab a damp cloth, but Officer Lynn stopped her.

"It's okay. The monitor is fine, just the way it is. Thank you." Officer Clarkson just chuckled. He knew how important this footage could be, but his partner was just so eager it was just funny to him.

"What are you laughing at?"

"Oh, nothing," Officer Clarkson said, putting his hands up. "Let's just finally watch this surveillance footage."

"It better be nothing," Officer Lynn replied with a smirk.

There had been some folding chairs leaning against the far wall. Officer Clarkson grabbed two, and they both took a seat in front of the monitor.

"Let me know if there's anything else I can do for you," Marie said.

"Okay. Will do. Right now, we're all set. Thank you," Officer Clarkson replied.

Marie just smiled and left the room. Right now, the two officers were sitting in a very quiet and private room inside the police station. It was sometimes used for storage, but it was pretty empty at the moment.

Emily automatically assigned herself to be in control of playing back the footage. Derek was anxious to see it too, but he just leaned back and let Emily do her thing. She didn't seem to know where to start first.

"So I'll start about fifteen minutes before the robbery takes place," she said more to herself than to Derek.

"Sounds good," he said.

The time stamp on the footage said 9:45 p.m. Emily could see two employees on the screen now. She could make out Chuck standing by the registers easily but couldn't quite make out the second employee.

The second employee had his back turned to this specific camera angle. Emily knew she could look at the footage from other angles, but something told her not to. She leaned forward for a better look.

"Do you see something?" Derek was curious.

"I think I recognize that second employee. He just needs to turn around," Emily said without taking her eyes off the monitor. This employee seemed to be stocking shelves or at least doing a quick touch-up.

"We could look at another angle," Derek suggested.

"Not yet. Just give it time."

Right now, nothing suspicious was going on. Nothing seemed out of the ordinary. Emily just couldn't look away from that employee.

Just then the unidentified employee started to turn around. He had only turned sideways when Emily paused the footage.

"That can't be right! Oh my god, no!" Emily said, putting her hand over her mouth.

"I'm going to say by that reaction that you do recognize him!" Derek seemed surprised and also leaned forward in his chair.

Emily seemed to have forgotten that Derek was sitting next to her. Her eyes were frozen on the young male on the monitor.

"No, no, no…" Emily shook her head and was starting to get upset. She played the footage now, waited until the employee was fully facing the camera, and she paused it again.

"He couldn't have been a part of this!" Emily was both shocked and a little upset.

"Tell me who that is. I need to know," Derek said, pointing to the monitor. Emily turned her head and slowly made eye contact with Derek.

"That's my son."

CHAPTER 27

"I WOULD ASK IF YOU'RE kidding, but I can tell that you're not," Derek said in shock. He honestly didn't know how to react after Emily told him she recognized her own son on the surveillance footage. He was at a total loss for words.

"Maybe it's nothing, you know. It tells you what Speedway he works at. The rest could be a coincidence."

"He was raised better than that. I know that for sure." Emily was looking down at her lap and rubbing her hands on her knees. "That can't be right."

"I'm not sure what to say right now," Derek started. "But I'm here for you," he said, placing his hand on her shoulder.

Out of nowhere, Emily shot up out of her chair. She started pacing the room. Derek just gave her some time and space and kept quiet.

"Oh my god, Derek, please don't tell anyone about this. And I mean not a single person!" Emily was now standing in the middle of the room.

"I won't tell a soul. I honestly feel that it is not my place to say anything at all."

"Good. Thank you." Emily seemed to be able to relax a little.

"Of course. Do you think that maybe we should continue to watch the rest of the footage? At least up until your son leaves. As of this point, he hasn't done anything wrong," Derek suggested.

"Yeah. Sure." Emily was still uneasy about it. Derek could tell. Emily walked back to her chair and sat down. She gave Derek a nervous look and then faced the monitor.

Both Emily and Derek were paying very close attention to Larry now that they almost forgot about Chuck. Emily never took her eyes off Larry. Derek was watching both Chuck and Larry. Chuck just seemed to be watching the time; he kept looking at the clock. Other than that, Chuck wasn't doing much of anything.

Larry continued to touch up the shelves to make things look nice. He seemed to be looking at his phone a lot too. Emily wasn't sure if that meant anything. Things seemed to shift a little bit though right when the time stamp on the footage read 10:00 p.m. Emily and Derek both saw Chuck look at Larry, and Chuck appeared to say something.

"Okay. Maybe Chuck is telling him to leave," Derek said.

"Maybe," Emily replied, not taking her eyes off the screen. "That would explain why Chuck was alone but not why the door was left unlocked."

They both continued to watch the screen. It did appear that Chuck was telling Larry to leave. Larry went to the back and was gone for a couple of minutes. He came back wearing his jacket, and it appeared that he was texting someone.

"See how he's holding his phone," Derek asked, pointing to the screen. "He's looking down at it like he's sending a text."

"Don't jump to conclusions," Emily shot back.

"Come on. You have to admit that much, Emily."

"Not necessarily." She looked at Derek now. "I don't like this at all. That's my son. He could be an accomplice to a robbery. You couldn't possibly know how I feel right now." Emily was clearly upset, and her voice was shaky.

"I'm sorry," Derek said in a very sincere voice.

Emily didn't seem to hear him. She just kept watching the screen.

Larry put his phone into his pocket, walked past Chuck, and walked outside. Larry left a door unlocked.

CHAPTER 28

IT HAD BEEN TWO DAYS since JoJo, Mackenzie, Larry, and Rachael had met at Subway. Rachael had relaxed some. She was still nervous about being caught on camera. Her main concern was Larry. He didn't wear a mask. He could easily be identified. There was no going back now.

Rachael was at home, sitting on her bed. She was on her phone, checking her Facebook for any new notifications. There were just a few, but none that interested her. Rachael got a vibe from JoJo that he would be the type of person who would post something on Facebook about the robbery. She kept that feeling to herself. He just wasn't involved, so he had the freedom to talk about it. She felt that he would. She had just met the guy, so she wasn't too sure about him. Right then, she got a text from him. Coincidence?

The text read, "Hey, are you busy?"

"Not really," she replied.

He responded to her text almost immediately.

"Awesome! Wanna meet up tonight? I know something we can all do to clear our heads."

Rachael paused at that. She wasn't sure what to say. Then another text came in.

"Don't worry. Larry already agreed to hang out." That made Rachael smile. She would feel more comfortable having Larry around.

"Okay, sure. What's the plan?" Rachael responded.

"We meet at my place. I'll text you my address. We can meet at my place at 8:00 p.m."

"Okay. What about Mackenzie?"

"Go ahead and invite her too." Rachael felt both nervous and excited about this, but she didn't know why. She was willing to do anything to distract herself. So she was focused on the positive and looked forward to hanging out with her friends later. After all, what could possibly go wrong?

CHAPTER 29

"WE NEED SOME SORT OF cool group name, ya know?" JoJo said with a smirk. "Like 'the cool kids' or something like that. It will be pretty cool, I think."

Larry, Mackenzie, and I all met at JoJo's at 8:00 p.m., and we were all sitting in the living room.

"Why do we need that?" I asked.

"Oh, come on, Rachael. Don't be like that! Let's have some fun." JoJo seemed overexcited about wanting a group name.

"It would be kind of fun to do that." Larry chuckled. "There's no harm in that."

"That's the spirit, bro!" JoJo jumped up from his chair. "Love it!"

"Boys will be boys," Mackenzie said, smiling and looking over at me.

"Come on, ladies, it won't do any harm. It could even turn into something cool." JoJo winked at us.

"Fine, but it better not be anything stupid," Mackenzie said, still smiling.

"Oh, don't worry. It won't be, I promise," JoJo assured her.

"So you wanted us to come over to clear our heads by coming up with a group name?" I asked sarcastically.

"Nope. I thought of the group name thing afterward," JoJo said proudly.

"What was the original plan?" Larry asked. "I'm curious."

"Can't tell you. Nope, we need a name first." JoJo was really into this group name. The three of us just laughed. It was a really good laugh. I think it helped all of us relax. I know it was helping me. I loved it.

"So, Rachael, are you in too?" JoJo asked. "You know you want to."

"Fine," I replied, rolling my eyes.

"Awesome!" JoJo seemed so thrilled that we all agreed to it. JoJo sat back down and seemed to be thinking or overthinking about what our group name would be.

"So nothing stupid. Got it." He smiled at Mackenzie. She just gave him a smirk back.

"How about the rebels?" Larry asked, smiling at me.

"Very funny. That only works for me, idiot," I shot back.

"She's right." Mackenzie agreed.

"I was joking." Larry put his hands up. "Easy."

"Oh, I got it," JoJo shot back up again. "The crazies! 'Cause you guys were crazy to do what you did!" JoJo clapped his hands together. Mackenzie rolled her eyes and shook her head. Larry was just laughing.

"Yes, it was crazy, and it was a thrill, but that name won't work. We worked more like a crew than anything." I chuckled.

"That's it!" JoJo was super excited and pointed to me.

"That's what?" I asked.

"The Crew. That's our group name."

CHAPTER 30

SO WE ALL DECIDED TO call our group The Crew. It made JoJo crazy excited, which made the rest of us laugh. It made all of us happy. Something so simple was able to help clear my mind and distract me, at least for the time being. It was a great feeling.

"So what was your plan? Why did you really ask us to hang out?" Larry asked.

"Did you three notice how there's a wooded area at the end of the block?" JoJo asked, looking at each of us.

"Yeah. What about it?" Mackenzie asked, now curious. I was even wondering where JoJo was going with this.

Larry had given Mackenzie and me a ride to JoJo's. We did notice the woods at the end of the block, but we didn't think much of it.

"We gotta check it out," JoJo said, rubbing his hands together.

"At night?" Larry asked. His eyes got pretty big.

"Oh, hell yeah! It will be creepy as hell and damn near pitch-black! It just sounds awesome! What do you think?"

"You're crazy!" Mackenzie almost shouted.

"I'm crazy?" JoJo replied, pointing to himself and staring at Mackenzie. "I'm not the one who robbed Speedway!" he said with a smirk.

"Good point, but aren't we supposed to forget about that right now?" Mackenzie shot back.

"Yes, we are," Larry stepped in. "But why go into the woods at night?" he now asked JoJo.

"I already told you, bro! Plus, we can see who gets scared easily!" JoJo chuckled.

"You have a warped sense of humor, man." Larry chuckled. "But what the hell. I'm in. Why not?"

"Awesome! What about you, two ladies? You're not scared, are you?" Mackenzie and I looked at each other, trying to determine what the other person was thinking.

"You know what? Screw it. I'll do it too. I like to believe that I don't scare easily," I said, looking at JoJo.

"Yes! I love it!" JoJo pumped his fist into the air.

"Well? Mackenzie?" Larry asked.

"I kind of feel like I have to now." She chuckled. "But if anyone scares me, I will beat you."

"Oh my god, yes! I'm so pumped right now! This is gonna be so awesome!" JoJo was acting like an excited little kid on Christmas morning.

"So get ready, guys! Let's get going!" JoJo said.

"You mean right now?" Mackenzie asked, a little bit nervous now.

"Well, yeah! Why wait? The sooner, the better!" JoJo said, smiling and rubbing his hands together.

"He kind of has a point," Larry said, looking at Mackenzie.

"Fine. Let's go!" Mackenzie said, getting up from her chair and heading for the door. "I don't need to put up with this. I got this." I just laughed. Mackenzie and JoJo were all fired up and ready to go, and here I was, still sitting on the couch, laughing.

Larry stood up from his chair and walked over to me with a smile. He just held out his hand, and I took it. He helped me up.

"Let's go have some fun," he said.

"Sounds like a plan." I smiled back.

CHAPTER 31

IT WAS AROUND 9:00 P.M. The police station seemed pretty quiet. There were other officers there, but Officer Lynn didn't seem to notice them. She was sitting at her desk with her feet up, and she was playing with a pen. She was also very distracted. It had been two long days since she recognized her own son, her own flesh and blood, on the surveillance footage from Speedway. Once the footage showed Larry leaving, she didn't even bother watching the rest. Derek did instead. The story that Chuck told them seemed to match the footage, but it was also very hilarious to Derek to watch it play out. He told Emily she should watch it too. That it would give her a good laugh and that it might make her feel better. She had no intention of seeing any more than she already had. Derek understood.

It was a Wednesday night. Emily could be home relaxing but was once again at work. It was much different this time. Only Emily and Derek knew about her son in the footage. Emily knew she had to do something about it, but she didn't know what. Was she supposed to call Larry's dad? Was she supposed to call Larry and question him? She never could have imagined she would be put in a situation like this. But there she was. She was so distracted by her own thoughts that she didn't hear Derek walk up to her.

"Holy shit!" Emily shouted and jumped with Derek, placing his hand on her shoulder.

"I'm sorry. I didn't mean to scare you. I called your name twice."

"Really? I guess I zoned out." Emily put her feet on the floor and leaned forward.

"I could only imagine," Derek replied. "We just got a call about a disruption not too far from here. Just wondering if maybe you would want to ride along."

"Do you know what it's about? I really could use a distraction," Emily said, now sitting up.

"From what I understand, a group of kids thought it would be cool to go out into a wooded area at night. It sounds like they're scaring people," Derek started. "Someone reported hearing firecrackers and screams at one point."

"Do people live near there?" Emily was curious.

"There are houses on one side and apartments on the other side. I believe the calls were made from multiple people living in the apartments."

"Let's check it out. It sounds interesting," Emily said, getting up and grabbing her jacket.

"Let's go," Derek replied.

CHAPTER 32

SO HERE WE WERE, THE Crew, out in the woods after dark like crazy people. We only had the flashlights from our cell phones. JoJo didn't plan ahead for this, so he didn't even think about needing flashlights. Idiot. It really was almost pitch-black. When we would hear a twig snap, we would all jump like a bunch of chickens. Then we would hope it was just an animal.

"We are all so damn jumpy. It's a totally different feeling when you're actually out here," JoJo said, looking at each of us. His voice sounded shaky.

"Are you scared?" I asked.

"Nope. Not me, no way," he replied so fast that it made me believe he really was scared.

Larry and JoJo were leading the way. Mackenzie and I were following right behind them. I kept looking behind me because I felt like I was being watched. We were on a trail, so I thought I would hear footsteps or hear something if someone was behind me.

"You need to stop looking behind you because you're really creeping me out," Mackenzie said, sounding scared. She actually stopped walking, turned around, and aimed her flashlight the way we just came.

"I don't see anything. Do you?" she asked me. I walked up next to her, aiming my flashlight in the same direction.

"I really can't see very far, but no. I don't see anything," I replied.

"So what's wrong?" she asked.

"I just have this feeling that I'm being watched."

"I'm gonna beat you if you keep talking like that," she said, sounding scared. Larry and JoJo had noticed that we had stopped. They didn't get too far, but they walked back to us.

"What's up? Is everything all right?" Larry asked us calmly.

"Rachael is freaking me out."

"I'm not trying to," I said, looking at Mackenzie.

"Did you hear something unusual? How is she freaking you out?" JoJo asked. His voice was shaky.

"She has a feeling that she's being watched," Mackenzie said to JoJo, but she was looking at me.

"It could be a deer," Larry said. "It could be nothing." He was trying to be comforting.

"I don't like the sound of that," JoJo said.

"Really, dude? This was your idea, and you're the one getting scared?" Larry seemed to be the calm one of the group.

"Don't try to give me crap, bro. It's totally different when you're actually out here," JoJo repeated.

"You already mentioned that," I said.

"Well, it's true," he said.

"Okay, fine. I have a plan. How about we all stand completely still and not make a sound and see if we hear anything odd," Larry suggested.

"That might actually make me feel better," I replied.

"Okay, then. Rachael is in. Anyone else?" Larry asked.

JoJo and Mackenzie aimed their flashlights at each other so they could see the look on the other person's face. They both had looks of hesitation. I couldn't blame them.

"If we all stay close together, then I'll do it," Mackenzie said.

"Same," JoJo agreed.

"All right, let's do it. No moving or talking. Flashlights off," Larry said. One by one, we all turned our flashlights off. It was damn near pitch-black. The only light we had was the moonlight.

I felt Mackenzie grab my arm. She had a strong grip. I knew she was really creeped out. So I held her arm. There was total silence for a while. Then we heard the sound of crickets. I thought that was pretty peaceful. The next sound wasn't so peaceful.

I heard the sound of multiple twigs breaking and the sounds of leaves being stepped on. Just out of habit, I started looking around even though I couldn't see anything in the darkness. *Please just be a deer*, I thought. The sounds sounded more like footsteps! They were coming closer to us! Mackenzie tightened her grip on my arm, and I squeezed her back. I wanted so badly to scream, but I held it in. Instead, I tried to take a deep breath as quietly as I could. That really didn't seem to help. The sounds seemed closer now. They seemed to be coming right toward Mackenzie and me.

"Fuck this," JoJo whispered. He turned his cell phone flashlight back on and aimed it right toward Mackenzie and me. Right when he did, we all let out terrifying screams!

CHAPTER 33

"WHAT THE FUCK! WHAT THE fuck! What the fuck!" JoJo was totally freaking out and also the only one who could actually speak at the moment. We all just took off running with no clue where we were going. We were all just following the light from JoJo's phone, his very bouncy light.

I was listening for any noise from behind us but couldn't make anything out over our own noise. Even though we were running on the trail, we were still crunching leaves and twigs. We just kept on running. We saw an apartment complex; we ran into the parking lot, where there was a lot more light. Then we all stopped to catch our breath. After a few minutes, it was Larry who spoke first.

"What the hell was that?" He had huge eyes and was holding his chest to help catch his breath.

"It was a damn werewolf! That's what it was!" JoJo shouted.

"It was more like someone dressed in all black wearing a very realistic werewolf mask and just standing there," Mackenzie said. Her voice was pretty shaky.

"Who the hell does that?" JoJo asked, scared as hell but trying to calm himself down.

"Someone who is screwed up in the head," I replied.

"That was intense, guys!" JoJo said. "We should head back."

"Um, how? We gotta go back the way we came. That jerk could still be there," Mackenzie said, pointing toward the woods.

"Shit, I'm not going back in there!" JoJo said, looking back into the woods. "No damn way!"

"I'm with you," I agreed. I was also holding my chest. My heart was pounding like crazy.

"So now what?" Larry asked.

"We'll figure it out, I guess. We need to," I replied. I didn't know what else to say. Before anyone could say anything else, there was a loud noise coming from the woods. We all spun around and looked into the darkness.

The noise sounded like fireworks, but we couldn't actually see them. We could sure hear them.

"Those damn kids are at it again! Call the police!" a man said from behind us. It made me actually scream a little.

Now we all turned to face the man who was talking. He had to be in his forties. He was very angry.

"That damn group of college kids think it's so funny to go into the woods at night and cause issues!" he said, almost shouting. We didn't know if he was talking to us or not. So we all just stood there, not knowing what to do. The man stood in his spot looking into the woods for a few moments then walked inside.

"So that solves that," JoJo said. "It's just college kids."

"But it's still crazy and scary!" Mackenzie said.

"Do you think he's calling the cops?" I asked Larry.

"I think he is. Especially with that attitude."

"I don't want to be around if the cops do show up! We gotta go! Like right now!" JoJo said, starting to panic. "I don't want to get blamed for this!"

"None of us do!" I shouted to JoJo. Mackenzie and Larry just shook their heads. What we didn't know was that the cops had already been called. Not until we saw two squad cars pull into the parking lot behind us.

"Mother...no way, bro!" JoJo shouted. He took off, running right back toward the woods. I just followed him. I'd rather be in the dark woods than get blamed for something that I didn't do. I stopped to turn back and look for Larry and Mackenzie. They were both just frozen in place!

"Guys, come on!" I shouted. Mackenzie seemed to snap out of it and ran toward me.

"I really don't want to go back in there!" She was literally shaking.

"I know, but do you want to face the cops?" I asked.

"Hell no!" Then she ran ahead of me toward the woods. JoJo and Mackenzie ran into the woods together. They didn't go in too far because I could see their flashlights turn on. I looked back to see if Larry was coming.

"Come on!" I shouted. Larry had only moved a few feet before I heard a female voice.

"Larry! Is that you?" the voice shouted.

CHAPTER 34

LARRY JUST FROZE IN PLACE. He knew that voice. He didn't want to believe that it could be her. It was. He knew that the voice belonged to his mom.

"Fuck," he whispered to himself. He looked toward the woods and could still see Rachael. He mouthed the word "run!" She seemed to understand because she disappeared into the dark woods.

"Larry?" his mom shouted again. He had his back turned when the squad cars pulled in. Now he slowly turned to face his mom. He could see she had a look of disbelief on her face. The man who was driving had to be her partner since he seemed to be in total shock.

"This isn't what you think," Larry said to his mom. She was starting to walk toward him now. Larry just stayed where he was. She stopped about ten feet away from him.

"I'm not sure what to think," she said softly. "Care to fill me in?" she asked, crossing her arms.

"I'm really not sure what to say right now." Larry really was at a loss for words.

"Okay, let me help you. We got multiple complaints from this apartment complex about screams and sounds of fireworks from these woods. Do you know anything about that?" She seemed very serious now. She was in full cop mode now.

"I know a little bit," Larry replied. Then he told her all about how he and his friends were out in the woods and told her what had happened to them.

"So where are your friends now?" she asked.

"I honestly don't know," he said, shrugging his shoulders. He thought that there might be a chance that they were in the woods waiting for him.

"Okay, then. Sounds like you and your friends weren't at fault," she started. "But there is something else that I need to talk to you about."

"What?" Larry asked, looking confused.

"I think you already know what," she replied, raising her eyebrows. Larry had an idea about what she was talking about. He was also hoping that he was wrong.

"What are you talking about? I told you what happened tonight," he said, playing dumb.

"That's not what I'm talking about," she replied seriously, still in full cop mode.

"So what then?" Larry was now nervous.

"Well." She started taking a step forward. "I didn't know what Speedway you worked at, but I do now."

Holy shit! That was Larry's first thought. He was literally speechless now. He was frozen in place.

"I think you and I need to talk," his mom said. "Let's take a ride to the station."

CHAPTER 35

EMILY AND DEREK HAD DRIVEN back to the station with Larry riding in the back seat. Nobody had said a word during the entire drive. Now Emily was sitting at her desk, facing her son. She had pulled a chair up next to her desk and had told him to sit down.

"So do you know why you're here?" Emily asked Larry.

"No, not really. You mentioned Speedway earlier, but that doesn't really mean anything," he said calmly. Emily always knew him to be calm.

"I did mention that. I also called you about it. You just failed to mention that you work at the one that got robbed," she replied.

"So. Is that a problem?" Larry asked, looking annoyed now.

"We'll see. I'm not quite sure yet." Emily was wondering if Larry knew something that she didn't.

"What are you talking about?"

"My partner and I talked to the manager, and we also saw the surveillance footage." She started studying Larry closely now. "I'm just going to say it. I saw you, Larry." Emily saw a look of shock appear on Larry's face, but it quickly disappeared.

"Well, I work there, so you would see me. I did work that night. I have nothing to hide." He seemed a tad bit nervous now.

"Okay. So tell me something. Why did you leave the door unlocked when you left?"

"Did I? I didn't mean to!" Larry seemed surprised. Emily couldn't tell if it was a lie or the truth.

"Yeah, it was left unlocked. Within minutes after you left, two young ladies robbed the store."

"I know about that. Everyone working there knows about that," Larry said. He just seemed to shrug it off like it was nothing.

"If there's anything you want to tell me, now would be the time," Emily said, leaning back in her chair.

"Nope. There's nothing."

"Nothing at all?" she asked.

"Nope."

"I know you and I don't have the greatest mother-and-son relationship, but—"

Larry cut her off. "Are you serious right now? There's no relationship. You choose your job over me!" Larry shouted, which got the attention of other officers, including Derek.

"You know what? I can't do this! I accidentally left the door unlocked. If you want to accuse me of something, you go right ahead. I gotta go." Larry got up so fast that the chair he was sitting in was tipped over.

"Larry, wait…" Emily got up and tried to reach for him, but he just pulled away and headed for the exit. Other officers looked as if they were about to attempt to stop him, but Emily just shook her head no.

"Just let him go."

Derek walked up next to Emily and put his hand on her shoulder.

"I'm sorry about that," he said softly.

"It's not your fault," she said, sitting back down. "I've always been more of a cop than a mom."

"You just don't know what to do in this case, that's all," Derek said softly. "Did you make any progress?"

"No. This case might just be a dead end," she said, taking a deep breath.

"That happens sometimes," he said, trying to be comforting. "We can't always win them all."

CHAPTER 36

"WHAT THE HELL? I WANNA know what happened to Larry!" JoJo was pulling on his hair in a panic now.

We all had gone back into the dark woods where the three of us had been hiding behind some trees. We watched as a female officer walked up to Larry. We watched them talk and even watched as they got into the squad car. The second squad car just followed them out of the apartment complex parking lot. Mackenzie and JoJo had their flashlights on but, at times, had to put their hands over the light so nobody could see us. We quickly made our way back through the woods and hoped the college kids were gone, even though Larry was our main focus. We ended up back at JoJo's house.

"I'm sure one of us will hear from him. Plus, his car is still here. He's gonna have to come back for that," I said, trying to stay positive.

"That's true," JoJo said, releasing his hair. "He does need to come back."

"But that could be tomorrow for all we know," Mackenzie said, falling back into a chair.

"Well, technically, it is tomorrow," JoJo replied, looking at his phone.

"What?" I asked, looking at my own phone. It was 12:02 a.m.

"My parents are gonna go off the wall if they notice I'm not home!" Now I was the one freaking out.

"Aren't you supposed to be a rebel now?" JoJo chuckled. "Just forget about them right now," he said, waving a hand at me.

"It's hard to honestly. You're right though," I said, trying to relax myself.

"Focus on Larry. If they do call, just let it go to voice mail," JoJo replied.

"It's not that easy. You don't know her parents," Mackenzie said.

"I'm honestly more focused on Larry. Can we go back to that, please?" JoJo asked.

"Sure, but first, are your parents even home?" Mackenzie asked JoJo.

"My mom is working overnight at the hospital, and my dad went off to visit his sister. So back to Larry," he said, sitting on the couch.

"That had to have been his mom. She said his name and recognized him with his back facing her," I said. It was more like thinking out loud.

"Damn. I forgot about that part. I'm dumb," Mackenzie said, slapping her forehead.

"He could be in deep now if he got caught on the cameras," JoJo said, staring directly at me.

"Let's hope not."

"There's really nothing we can do for him at this point. We can only wait for him to contact us," Mackenzie said softly.

We all just sat in silence for a while, knowing what Mackenzie said was true. Then out of nowhere, I felt my phone vibrate. It was a text from Larry.

"I just got a text from Larry!" I was pretty excited.

"What's it say?" Mackenzie asked. She seemed pretty nervous too.

"Meet me back at JoJo's. I'll be there soon."

CHAPTER 37

LARRY HAD MET US AT JoJo's about thirty minutes later. He had to use Uber to get from the police station to JoJo's. He seemed to be pretty annoyed, so we really didn't say anything. Larry gave Mackenzie and me a ride back home and said he would talk to all of us the next day.

"So did your parents know you got home late last night?" Mackenzie asked. She seemed a little concerned. She and I were actually sitting at the park by my house, waiting for Larry and JoJo to show up.

"Actually, no. I got home and found a note on the kitchen table from my mom. It said she got a call late last night from my uncle that my grandpa is sick and that she and my dad had to leave right away." I know I sounded concerned and annoyed at the same time.

"What the hell? Are you serious?" she asked, even though she knew I was.

"Yeah! I tried calling them this morning, but no answer."

"That doesn't sound like your parents at all! I hope your grandpa is okay."

"So do I. Now I'm going to be worried until I hear from them."

"No news is good news, right?" Mackenzie looked at me with a slight smile.

"Sure." Just then we saw Larry's car pull up. We both headed over to meet the guys at the car.

We headed to a nearby table where Larry had filled us in on what happened the night before.

"So as far as I'm concerned, we got away with it," Larry said with a smile, slapping the table.

"So you lied? And your mom just believed you?" Mackenzie kind of looked confused.

"Don't question it. Go with it!" JoJo said then started to laugh.

"I'll for sure go with it!" I said with a smile.

"See, there you go! Rachael has the right idea." JoJo smiled.

"I mean, it was a crazy, insane, and dumb idea," I admitted. "But it was a thrill."

"What did I tell you!" Larry smiled.

"We should be celebrating, guys!" JoJo said, standing up.

"Just hold on a second," Larry said. "There's no rush."

"Don't be a party pooper, bro!" JoJo shouted like he was pouting like a child but then laughed. Larry couldn't help but laugh too.

"Well, if you guys are interested, my parents are out of town. We can hang out at my house tonight," I suggested.

"I'm up for that," Mackenzie said. "Maybe have some pizza and make it a movie night."

"Sure, why not?" JoJo agreed.

"What time?" Larry asked.

"We can make it at six," I said. "Let's do more than that."

"Like what?" JoJo asked, looking kind of confused.

"Well, we are The Crew, right? Maybe we should start acting like it."

CHAPTER 38

"SO LET ME GET THIS straight. Your parents are out of town, so you decide to turn your house into a base camp?" JoJo asked, a little confused. "Does that sound about right?"

"Pretty much. I'm going to say it's safe to officially say we got away with the Speedway robbery, but what if it's only our first? I have this itch to do more. Like the one just isn't enough," I said with a little spunk. The four of us were standing around my kitchen table now, looking at my setup.

We all left the park around two thirty, so I had time to set something up before they arrived at six. After robbing Speedway, I had this itch to do more. I just couldn't move forward until we were in the clear. This was my chance.

My setup consisted of four notebooks, four pens, four pairs of thin black gloves that I had recently bought at the nearest Target, my one tube of pepper spray, my pocketknife, and the carry-on bag we had used before.

"What are you thinking this time?" Larry asked, looking nervous as if he was afraid to hear the answer.

"Maybe a little breaking and entering." It was more of a suggestion than a solid answer. Larry looked at me and just slightly shook his head.

"Stepping up your game, huh?"

"Shit, I'm in. I'll help plan it too!" JoJo was crazily excited. It was like he was on a sugar high.

"What do you need me to do?"

"Down, boy. Besides, she's kidding. It's a joke," Mackenzie said, looking from JoJo to me. "Right? You're joking?" She looked nervous too. I could only shake my head.

"Oh, come on! You're turning into quite the rebel!" she said, raising her voice.

"Maybe that's the point," I replied with a smirk.

"Your parents will find out. You do know that, don't you?"

"I'll worry about them."

"So you turn eighteen and get a little bit of freedom, and this is what you want to do with it?" Larry asked.

It was hard to read his expression. He seemed excited but worried at the same time.

"It feels right. It's hard to explain," I said, crossing my arms.

"That's what I'm talking about," JoJo replied, rubbing his hands together. "This sounds pretty exciting."

"It sounds like a crazy summer break to me," Mackenzie replied. "This is nuts. Doing it once is one thing, but to do it again is something totally different."

"You did it before. Are you going to chicken out?" JoJo asked, taunting her.

"I never said yes, and I never said no," she snapped back. JoJo started to make chicken noises, and Mackenzie slugged him pretty hard in the arm. Larry and I just laughed at it.

"So let's just back up a bit," I said, looking at Larry. "I don't think breaking and entering would be stepping up my game." Larry looked at me and smiled.

"Well, maybe not. I personally feel it could be less risky. I mean, if it's a private residence, who doesn't have all those new cameras all over their houses."

"Oh, I know places like that!" JoJo bounced up and down like a kid. He was even raising his hand.

"Why are you raising your hand? Are we back in class?" Mackenzie asked, giving JoJo an odd expression.

"I'm just getting overexcited!" JoJo shot back. "I watch a lot of TV and movies, okay. I can pull this stuff off!" JoJo said with pure confidence.

"Did you seriously just say that?" Mackenzie asked in a serious tone.

"Yup. TV and movies tell you what not to do. We'll just do the opposite and be just fine." JoJo exclaimed.

The three of us could only just stand there and wonder if he was serious or just joking.

"Dude, you're a dumbass," Larry said, breaking the silence.

"Whatever, bro. Watch me be right."

"Anyways, moving on. Are we going to watch any movies or not?" Mackenzie asked. "I wouldn't be upset if we don't."

"There are plenty of movies in the living room. Knock yourself out," I said.

"You know what, this has my attention. I'm more interested in this setup here," Larry said, smiling and then winking at me. I think I started to blush a little bit.

"Forget movies! Bro, I'm all over this!" JoJo said, rubbing his hands together again. So one by one, we all slowly turned to look at Mackenzie. She looked nervous, and we could tell she was hesitating.

"Okay, fine. Screw movies! Let's plan our next crime!"

CHAPTER 39

PLANNING MY SECOND CRIME SEEMED to be easier. This time, we had four people planning it instead of two. JoJo said he knew someone who just pissed him off constantly, so he wanted that person to be the target. That kind of scared me a little bit. I was also a little nervous when Larry and JoJo left to get snacks. To me, that meant that it could turn into a long night.

Actually, Larry helped plan our robbery but only played a small part. Now he wasn't afraid to be completely in on the action. Even though his own mom caught him on the surveillance footage, that didn't even seem to faze him anymore, which also scared me a little bit too.

"Okay, people, we got snacks and other crap," JoJo announced as he and Larry returned from the store. Larry followed him as he walked into the kitchen. They were both carrying bags of stuff.

"You got enough to feed a small army!" Mackenzie exclaimed. "Did you really need all that?"

"First of all, it's not all food. Second, I got other crap like I said," JoJo said with a sarcastic grin. JoJo set the bags on the free spot on the table and started to unpack them.

"We got some pepperoni pizza rolls, four boxes of chicken, two are buffalo and two are BBQ, then we got some cool ranch Doritos and nacho cheese Doritos. We got some chocolate doughnuts. Larry wanted the doughnuts." He looked up and gave Larry a smirk then went back to unpacking the bags.

"Next, we got flavored water which made the bags damn heavy. We got enough for each of us to have three. Have fun fighting over the different flavors." He started laughing at his own joke. While he kept naming off what they picked up, Mackenzie just looked at me, lipped the word "wow," and then smiled. JoJo just kept going.

"Now we got some pop that's still in the car. Oh, Mackenzie, you're gonna love this. We got some Mountain Dew just for you." He chuckled.

"Ha ha, very funny, smartass," she replied sarcastically and threw crumpled paper at him.

"I'd rather be hit with paper than pop." He was laughing pretty hard now. We all had to laugh at that one.

"But I'm not done. There's still more stuff. I didn't know what kind of things you guys liked, so I got a variety."

"He went a little crazy," Larry admitted. He had been standing in the kitchen doorway the entire time.

"Really, bro? You helped pick some of this stuff out! Anyways, back to the snacks. We also got Cheez Balls, Oreos, but just the regular Oreos. We got some cashews and some king-size candy 'cause there was a sale on those. I couldn't resist that. Plus pizza. You can never go wrong with pizza." JoJo looked at us with a huge grin.

"Okay then." I smiled, "So what else could you possibly have?"

"Oh, right! I got the mini version of Jenga! That could be fun. I got a Bop-it because I've always loved them, and I got a random ass slinky."

"Really? A random ass slinky?" I asked.

"Hell yeah! They're kind of cool," JoJo explained. "You know what, just leave me and my slinky alone," he said, hugging the slinky. Nobody knew what to say to that. We all busted out laughing.

"Whatever," JoJo said.

"Let's just plan our crime, shall we?" Larry asked, looking at me and raising one eyebrow. I just smiled.

"Come on, lover boy, you gotta fill us in on who has been pissing you off," Mackenzie said, sitting down at the table.

"Funny," JoJo replied. "All right. Where do I start?"

"It's not another big guy, is it? 'Cause we need to know that right now if it is," I said. I was very serious.

"Nope. Not this time. And I'm serious about that," JoJo answered. Before JoJo could get any further, Larry got a phone call. He reached into his pocket for his phone and looked shocked when he saw who was calling him.

"Who is it?" I asked.

"It's my dad. He rarely calls me. So this is weird," he said and then answered the phone. He was on the phone for a while, and the three of us just remained silent. Larry was getting agitated, so we assumed something was wrong. Soon Larry hung up and slammed his phone on the table.

"I can't believe her!"

"Who?" we all asked.

"My mom called my dad and told him everything that happened!"

CHAPTER 40

"I CAN'T BELIEVE THAT I did what I did," Emily said, looking out the window of the police station. Emily had made the decision to call Larry's dad and told him everything she knew about what had been going on with Larry.

"Erik thought that it was all a lie. That I was the one who wanted attention," Emily said, close to tears. Derek had been standing next to her, and once again, he didn't know what to say.

"He needed to know. I personally feel that I made the right decision," she said softly.

"It's not my place to say, but I think you were right to tell him," Derek said softly.

"Maybe he just didn't know how to react to it," Derek suggested.

"Maybe he couldn't accept the fact that Larry could be that kind of kid," Emily said, now facing Derek. "Larry may never speak to me again. I did consider that before I called his dad. I just want him to stay out of trouble."

"Maybe it really was an accident when Larry left that door unlocked. He wasn't the one causing the disturbances in those woods either," Derek said. "So he doesn't seem like a bad kid to me."

"You're right. I didn't think about it like that. I'm thinking more like a cop than a mom again," Emily said, taking a deep breath. "I told his dad, Erik, to keep an eye on him. Erik said he didn't need to. He said that he trusts Larry."

Emily got quiet for a while. She did trust Larry too. She just felt that she didn't know Larry as well as his dad did. Maybe that was true. She knew she couldn't change the past. If she could, she would fix all her mistakes. She would have spent so much more time with her family instead of letting it all fall apart. She knew that she would never forgive herself for any of it. Ever. But she also knew that she had to move forward, which was so much easier said than done.

Just then both Emily and Derek jumped at the sound coming from the room where they had watched the surveillance footage.

"Does that sound like laughter to you?" Derek asked, looking confused.

"Yeah. It does actually." Both of them headed toward the sound. Sure enough, it was the sound of laughter. There was a group of off-duty officers gathered in the small room with buckets of popcorn, watching the surveillance footage from Speedway.

"Oh my god, this is some of the funniest shit I've seen in a long time!" one officer said, pointing and laughing.

"My favorite part is when that guy gets beat with pop!" said another officer.

"Well, looks like the footage is therapeutic," Derek said with a smile, looking at Emily.

"Looks like it." She smiled back.

"Maybe you should watch it too. Maybe it will cheer you up." Derek smiled, pointing into the room.

"You never know. It just might," Emily replied with a smile.

"Trust me. It made me laugh." Derek chuckled.

"Maybe I'll watch it for just a minute," Emily said, walking into the room.

After seeing Larry in the footage, she couldn't pull herself together to be able to watch anymore. But by how hard the other officers were laughing, she couldn't help but watch it now. In no time, she was laughing too. The officers would rewind it and watch it over again. They couldn't get enough of it, and neither could she.

CHAPTER 41

SOME TIME HAD PASSED SINCE Larry got off the phone with his dad. He had informed the three of us what was said between his parents. He felt that his dad was on his side, but he felt a lot of anger toward his mom. We understood his anger, but at the same time, we could also understand why his mom had called his dad. This made me think that maybe we shouldn't do our breaking and entering like we were planning after all. Mackenzie and JoJo sat down at the table while Larry informed us on what was going on. They had remained there and kept pretty quiet ever since. Not sure what to do. Larry had gone over to sit on the couch. I wanted to talk to Larry, but I was unsure of what to say. I had never been in a situation like this before.

"Hey," I said softly as I slowly made my way over to Larry, and I also sat on the couch.

"Hey," he said, looking at me.

"So what happens now?" I asked.

"Not sure. Maybe I just need to pull myself together and move on."

"What do you mean?"

"Well, my mom clearly thinks I'm a bad guy, so why not be one?" He had a type of look in his eye that I just couldn't explain.

"I'm not really following you," I replied. I was pretty confused.

"My mom thinks I'm a bad guy when she doesn't have anything solid to hold against me. If she acted like a mom more, she would see that I don't do this kind of thing. Instead, she just jumps to conclusions and throws me under the bus."

"Okay. I'm kind of following you," I said, but still confused. "What are you getting at?"

"Let's do this breaking and entering thing. JoJo said he knows someone who has it coming. So screw my mom. I'm all in," Larry said, starting to get all pumped up.

"Are you sure you're thinking straight right now?" I asked, concerned.

"Maybe. Maybe not. Usually, this isn't how I act, but I'm getting a rush from all this, and I really like that feeling."

"I know exactly what you mean!" I replied. "I never knew I could feel so many emotions at once! From nervous to terrified then relief and success. It's hard to explain."

"Exactly!" Larry replied, clapping his hands together and turning his body to face me. He had a huge smile on his face now.

"Well, what do you say? Are you still in?"

"Well, it was my plan, so yeah. I'm still in!" I said, now smiling.

"Awesome. Let me go talk to JoJo and Mackenzie," Larry replied, now standing up. "But first, this is for you," he said, handing me a candy wrapper.

"What is it?" I asked, knowing I had an odd look on my face.

"Just read the inside and get back to me. You can take your time." He smiled and then walked into the kitchen to talk to JoJo and Mackenzie. I stayed on the couch and looked at the folded-up candy wrapper in my hand.

"Um, okay," I said quietly to myself as I slowly opened it. It turned out to be a note in fairly small writing that said, "Hey, I know this might be weird to write you a note on a candy wrapper, but I'm just too nervous to ask you this. I'm just really hoping that you will be my girlfriend. Do you want to go out sometime soon? Larry."

I had to read the note twice because I couldn't believe what I read the first time. I was so shocked and excited, and I knew my answer already. I just tried to control my emotions for the moment. The four of us had other things to focus on at the moment.

CHAPTER 42

"SO THIS GUY I MENTIONED is middle-aged. He does not have any security systems of any kind. He does not even have a dog. He bothers a lot of people in the neighborhood who do nothing but bitch about him." JoJo had started to tell us about this man who he felt had trouble coming his way.

"He is constantly watching people, like all the time. It doesn't even matter what you're doing!"

"Hold on a sec," Larry interrupted. "Did you just say neighborhood?"

"Yup. Is that a problem?" JoJo asked.

"So we're going to break into your neighbor's house?" Mackenzie asked, looking a little shocked.

"Yeah. I mean, how else would I know about this guy? Did I forget to mention he was my neighbor?" JoJo asked with a smug look on his face.

"Yes!" Mackenzie, Larry, and I all said in unison.

We were all sitting around the kitchen table at my place again. It was only 10:00 a.m., but we had already made a pizza and had snacks covering part of the table. It had been three days since my parents left to be with my grandpa. They had called to tell me he would be okay and that they would be home in a couple of days, which gave us a limited amount of time to make our plans.

"You always fail to mention something, you know that?" Mackenzie asked, leaning back in her chair and folding her arms.

"That's what makes it more exciting, don't you think?" JoJo said, laughing.

"No. Not really," I said very seriously. "First, it was Chuck, who happened to be a big guy. Now it's your neighbor."

"Actually, Rachael, I was the one who didn't tell you about Chuck," Larry corrected me.

Both Larry and JoJo started laughing at that. Mackenzie and I just looked at each other and rolled our eyes.

"You do realize we have a limited amount of time to plan this, right? My parents will be home in a couple of days!" I said, a little bit irritated.

"Yeah, yeah. It won't be a problem," JoJo said, waving me off. "I got more to tell you about this dude." He reached over to grab a notebook and a pen from the center of the table.

"So let me draw you a quick map of his front yard. First of all, he has no fence around his front yard. So maybe we can peek in through a front window to find a way in," JoJo said as he started to draw a quick map. He drew an outline of what appeared to be a house and two shapes of what appeared to be trees.

"Are those trees?" Mackenzie asked.

"Yup. In case we need to hide behind them for any reason. One is a willow tree. It would be easy to hide behind that." JoJo continued to add to the map by adding a garage to the left of the house. "This guy does not have an attached garage, so that could be a pro for us."

"Okay. I'm following you so far, but why do people bitch about this guy?" Larry asked.

"Oh, right. It's because he's always watching you. Like he doesn't believe people need their privacy. He gets mad at other neighbors if they let their grass grow too long. He's very anal about the property line. Like if you accidentally cross it, he yells at you for trespassing! Plus, if tree twigs or leaves fall on his yard, he gets very upset!"

"Really? This guy sounds like a joke," Mackenzie said. "I wouldn't be able to live next to someone like that."

"Exactly," JoJo said, pointing a finger at her. "He calls the cops on anyone for anything! He's known for reporting false crap!"

"Which makes this easier," Larry said with a smirk, "Some cops may not respond to someone like that. I mean, I could be wrong, but maybe I'm right."

I had slowly leaned forward in my chair and now had my arms folded on the table. I had been listening closely and felt that this guy really did have this coming.

"So what are you thinking, JoJo?" I asked, "Do we do this while the guy is sleeping? Or wait until he leaves?"

"Well, I happen to know that he leaves town every weekend," JoJo answered with a smile. "We can do this Friday night!"

"Okay, so two things. Number one, when were you planning on telling us that he leaves town every weekend?" Mackenzie asked, sounding a little annoyed.

"Right now, I guess." JoJo looked at her and chuckled.

"You're unbelievable," Mackenzie said, rubbing her temples.

"Funny. So what's number two?" JoJo asked impatiently.

"Well, number two would be the fact that tomorrow is Friday!"

"Exactly!"

CHAPTER 43

EMILY WAS ONCE AGAIN SITTING at her desk with a cup of coffee in her hand. This time, she was staring at her computer screen at the latest police report that she had been asked to look at.

"This guy needs a life," she said to herself.

She was looking at a report that had been filed out a week ago for a Mr. Anthony Scott. The report said Mr. Scott was a middle-aged man who had called the police when a branch from a neighbor's tree had fallen into his yard. It stated that Mr. Scott felt that his neighbor was trying to dispose of their trash in his yard and that he did not contact his neighbor about it. He just called the police the minute he noticed it in a fit of rage.

"Wow," Emily said, rubbing her head with her free hand and putting her coffee down.

"Everything all right?" Derek asked, walking up to her.

"Remember Anthony Scott? The man who calls the police on his neighbors for anything and everything? I was just looking at the latest report on him," Emily said, looking at Derek and pointing at her computer.

"Please tell me you're not wasting your time on this guy. He's a joke," Derek said, looking at the report. "See? That right there is no reason to call the police. Just throw the branch away. Problem solved."

"True." Emily sighed a little bit.

"What's wrong?" Derek asked.

"I just feel bummed that the Speedway robbery was a bust. We didn't recover any money. The surveillance tape didn't give us any new info on the suspects. I mean, other than the fact that they also stole candy and scratch-offs." Emily sat back in her chair. "It's just hard to move on."

"I get it. You can't win them all," Derek said with a smile.

"True. All I know for sure is where Larry works," she replied.

"And that he is innocent as far as we're concerned," Derek added. "That's important."

"That's also true," Emily said, smiling, "and also very comforting."

"So are you checking out Anthony Scott as a way to move on to something new?" Derek asked, confused.

"I wouldn't say it's something new. This guy has been playing this game for as long as I can remember." Emily was pointing at the computer. "I was asked to look at it to confirm if it was real."

"So let me guess, the officer who responded to that call has never dealt with Mr. Scott before?" Derek asked. Now he laughed a little.

"Nope. First time. He thought someone from the department was playing a joke on him." Emily was looking at Derek with a smile.

"That would be mean but funny. I could see it happening to a rookie," Derek said, now laughing harder. Emily got up and lightly slapped his arm.

"As long as I'm not the one responding to those calls, I'll be just fine."

CHAPTER 44

SO AFTER JOJO TOLD US about how his neighbor leaves every weekend, I had to get some air. I just felt like everything was just happening so fast. It was a different feeling than robbing Speedway. This time, it felt more personal. Robbing Speedway was Larry's way of getting back at his boss, but now this. This was JoJo's chance to get back at his neighbor, and he seemed more than happy to do it. I just wasn't a fan of invading people's personal space, even though this was my idea.

Right now, I was outside alone, sitting on my front steps, just trying to relax and prepare myself for what would come next.

"Hey. You okay?" Mackenzie had walked up to me, and I didn't even hear her.

"Girl, you scared me!" I said, jumping a little.

"Sorry. I just wanted to check on you."

"I'm not sure how I feel. I mean, JoJo wants to do this tomorrow night!" I said, making eye contact with her. "I wasn't thinking it would happen so fast!"

"Same here! But if we turn back now, I don't think we will actually do it," she replied.

"Maybe. How do you feel about this?"

"It's another rush. It's a different level now, that's for sure. It might be easier since there are no cameras this time," she said.

"I'm for sure wearing all-black clothes again! That's for damn sure."

"Oh, hell yeah!" Mackenzie said with wide eyes. "The guy's better dress that way too!"

"I hope so. So speaking of the guys. I wanna tell you something about Larry," I said, trying to switch gears, even if it was for just a few minutes.

"All right. What's up?" she asked, sitting down next to me. I reached into my pocket and pulled out the candy wrapper.

"Read this," I said, smiling and handing her the wrapper.

"Am I supposed to see how much sugar was in the candy?" she asked, taking the wrapper and laughing.

"Just unwrap it and read what it says on the inside." I was now smiling. I watched her read the note and saw how big her eyes got.

"Oh my god!" she said. She was very excited. "He asked you out? I'm jealous! So what did you say?"

"I didn't answer him yet. I'll wait until Saturday. You know, after we mess with JoJo's neighbor," I said, still smiling.

"Well, you're gonna say yes, right? 'Cause if you don't date him, I will!" Mackenzie laughed.

CHAPTER 45

HAVE YOU EVER GOTTEN THE feeling that if you do a certain thing, something bad will happen? That if you could look into the future and see the results of something unfold, you would go back in time and not do it at all? I wish that was possible. If I had only known what was about to happen tonight during our next crime, I would have backed out immediately! I wouldn't care if it was my idea! I did have those thoughts, but I kept them to myself. Maybe it was just nerves. Maybe not. We were all in Larry's car and parked at the end of the block of the house we were about to break into.

We were all dressed in solid black. We even had on our solid black gloves. Mackenzie and I also had our hair pulled back.

Larry had also brought along the duffel bag that contained the money from the Speedway robbery. He had transferred the money from the duffel bag to a smaller bag that he had hidden in his attic. He was confident that it would be a great hiding place.

"So there it is. The third house on the right," JoJo said. "This is it, guys. Showtime."

"Wait just a sec," I said. "What's our first move?"

"Well, it's ten thirty right now. I would think a majority of the neighbors would be asleep by now. If not, they might be watching TV. So maybe we can just park the car here and casually walk up to the house," JoJo replied.

"Really? Do you really think it will be that easy?" Mackenzie asked.

"Yes. Actually, I do," JoJo said with pure confidence.

"Okay. Just one problem," I started. "Do you realize we are parked right by a streetlight?"

"Oh yeah. There's that," JoJo said.

"You know what? Let's just go. Instead of talking, let's just do this," Larry said, getting out of the car.

"Bro! Wait, man!" JoJo shouted, also getting out of the car. "Wait for me!"

Mackenzie and I quickly looked at each other, shrugged our shoulders, and followed the guys.

"Shhh!" Mackenzie said. "I'm sure someone heard us shutting all four car doors just now."

"Chicken." JoJo smiled.

"I'm serious, jerk! I'm just feeling uneasy right now!"

"We all are," I said, grabbing her shoulder.

"No. Seriously, guys. I hear a damn chicken!" JoJo exclaimed.

"Stop messing around, dude. Now is not the time," Larry said very seriously.

"Just be quiet and don't move. Just listen," JoJo said, holding a finger to his mouth, saying be quiet. It took a few moments, but in the silence, we did, in fact, hear the sounds of a chicken in the house we were standing by. It was just two houses away from our target.

"What the hell?" I said. "Who has chickens?"

"I don't know," JoJo whispered, "but it's kinda funny."

"It's a distraction," Larry said. "Let's just go."

"You're right, bro! Let's move," JoJo said, walking in front of Larry. "Fuck that chicken. We got work to do."

"Oh, brother," Larry said, looking at me. "He's a piece of work."

Before I could reply, I saw something small running fast out of the shadows and toward JoJo.

"Chicken!" JoJo screamed, and he started to run.

"Now that's hilarious!" Mackenzie said, pointing at JoJo and starting to laugh. We were all standing in the road, watching our friend get chased by some crazy chicken who must have broken out of its cage. All we could do was laugh.

"Help! It's not funny!" JoJo said in a type of panic, still running.

"I love this!" Mackenzie laughed some more.

"That looks like a mad chicken. I'm not going near that thing," Larry said.

"Not me!" I said, laughing and putting my hands up. "Not it."

"Shouldn't we do something before he attracts attention?" Mackenzie asked, now showing some concern.

"Probably," Larry and I said in unison.

"But do we really have to?" Larry asked, laughing.

"Hold on," I said. "Where'd he go?" It was all a sudden really quiet, and none of us could see or hear JoJo.

"What the hell? He was just here," Larry said, looking around. Then his cell phone buzzed. "It's a text from JoJo. He's at the house in the backyard."

"Really? Do we need to save him from a chicken?" Mackenzie asked, laughing. Larry chuckled.

"Let's just go. We need to get out of the street anyways," I said. So the three of us ran to the target house with the willow tree in front of the yard that JoJo had told us about and snuck around the side of the house and into the backyard.

"JoJo," Larry whispered, "where are you?"

"Over here, bro," JoJo said, coming out of a shed.

"Whoa, wait? Were you hiding in a shed from a damn chicken?" Mackenzie asked. She was laughing pretty hard now.

"Don't judge me. Don't you know chickens have sharp claws?"

Now Larry, Mackenzie, and I could no longer hold back our laughter.

"Shut up, okay! This wasn't part of the plan," JoJo said.

"Whatever you say," I replied.

"Good. Now let's just move on. Just a second." He stepped back into the shed and came out with a small board.

"What's that for?" I asked, confused.

"It's just in case that bastard chicken comes back. I don't know where it went."

"That's funny right there." Larry smiled.

"Bro, just shut up. I was just lucky that the shed wasn't locked."

"Yeah. Wonder why it was open," I said, looking at the shed.

"Who cares? Let's go," JoJo demanded.

"Chill, man. Let's just—" Larry got interrupted by a noise coming from some flower bushes behind us. We all whipped around to look in that direction. I made sure I had put my small flashlight in the inside pocket of my jacket before we left. I took it out now, turned it on, and aimed it toward the noise. I was frozen. I was nervous. I had so many emotions running through me that I didn't know what to do.

"It's that bastard chicken, bro. I just know it," JoJo said, raising the board.

"Are you gonna kill it if it is?" Mackenzie asked.

"Yup," JoJo replied, still staring at the bushes.

Just then, there was more noise and rustling coming from the bushes. Then sure enough, the chicken came out flapping its wings and seemed to be charging right at us. JoJo didn't miss a beat and stepped up toward the chicken, holding up the board.

"You bastard chicken!" Right then, the chicken flew up in the air right at JoJo. At the same time, JoJo swung the board and smacked the chicken.

"Holy shit, man!" Larry shouted. "Did you just kill it?"

"Bro, I don't know." JoJo dropped the board. He poked the chicken, who was now just lying there.

"Yup. It's dead," JoJo said. I saw the whole thing but was a little slow with keeping up. It all happened so fast.

"I just killed a crazy bastard chicken. That's what happened." JoJo smirked. "Now let's get into this damn house."

JoJo walked away from us and toward the house. The rest of us slowly followed him.

CHAPTER 46

EMILY WAS JUST GRABBING HER jacket and was about to head home after another late night at work when her desk phone started to ring.

"Really?" she asked, looking at the phone.

"Officer Lynn," Emily said but regretted answering the phone.

"Hello. Officer Lynn. This is Amanda Johnson. I just wanted to call in a complaint."

"Okay. Go ahead," Emily said, sitting down and grabbing a paper pad and a pen.

"Well, I called to complain about this neighbor before. His name is Anthony Scott," Amanda said calmly.

Oh, great, Emily thought. *Not again.*

"What's going on?" Emily asked.

"I see an unfamiliar car parked at the end of the block. It doesn't belong to anyone I know. It just seems very suspicious. I know Mr. Scott is out of town. I think someone may be at his house right now." Emily rubbed her tired eyes, and she wished she had let the phone ring.

"Why would you think that?" Emily asked.

"Well, he's not a friendly guy at all. It wouldn't surprise me if someone wanted to get back at him. I'm calling for my own safety."

"Okay. I do understand that. I'll let an officer know about this," Emily replied, even though she didn't want to waste time on this.

"Thank you."

"You're welcome. Be safe," Emily said and hung up the phone. Just then Emily realized that she hadn't asked about the car's description.

"Crap," she said out loud.

"Is something wrong?" Emily heard a voice behind her and whipped around in her chair.

"Easy. I didn't mean to scare you," Derek said.

"Um. Yeah, it's okay. I was just going to leave, then I got a call," Emily said.

"What was it?" Derek now seemed concerned.

"Another complaint about Mr. Scott. A neighbor spotted a suspicious car at the end of her block that she didn't recognize, and I didn't ask for any information about it," she replied, rubbing her eyes.

"It may be nothing," he started. "Let's just both call it a night and head home," he said.

"Sounds like a plan," she said, standing up. "I didn't even realize that it's almost eleven."

"Neither did I. Come on, let's—" Derek was interrupted by the phone ringing again.

"Just let it ring," Emily said, yawning.

"It could be something important," Derek replied.

"Officer Clarkson," Derek said, answering the phone.

"Oh, hi. This is Jason Pepper. I'm calling about some suspicious activity on my block."

"Okay. Can you tell me what's going on, sir?"

"Oh yes. There's a dark-colored car parked at the end of the block that I've never seen before. Earlier, I had heard car doors slamming shut, so I looked outside and saw four people dressed in all black. Usually, I mind my own business, but the car is still there, and I don't like this."

"Could you tell me your address?" Derek asked. He was also writing this down, and Emily was reading it as fast as she could, not wanting to miss a beat.

"Sure, 1600 Winston Lane N. I'm a neighbor of Anthony Scott. I only mention him because I've seen officers here before. I'm sure you know the area."

"Yes, we do," Derek replied. He wrote Anthony Scott on the paper for Emily to see.

"Another one?" she whispered.

"Do you know anything else? Were you able to recognize anyone?"

"No, Officer, I didn't recognize anyone. It's too dark. One of them was carrying some sort of bag, if that means anything."

"That's helpful. Thank you. What about the car?" Derek asked.

"Well, these people weren't too smart. The car is parked next to the streetlight. It looks like a Ford Fusion to me. It's some darker color."

"Okay, that's helpful. Thank you. Do you have any more information?" Derek asked.

"No, Officer. I'm afraid that's it."

"Okay. Thank you, sir. Have a nice night," Derek replied then hung up the phone.

"So that's two calls in a matter of minutes. It's not Mr. Scott calling himself now over dumb things. I think something might be going on. I think it's worth checking out," Derek said seriously.

"Maybe. Let's go take a look," Emily said.

"Let's go."

CHAPTER 47

"SO FROM NOW ON, WE need to be quiet! Do you guys understand? No more laughing. I don't know about you three, but I don't want to get caught!" Larry was very serious and a little demanding.

"Will you chill, bro? We're all good," JoJo replied with a smirk.

"You don't know that for sure. I have a really bad feeling right now," Larry said, looking around. We were all still in the backyard of Anthony Scott's house. We had moved closer to the house, and we were now looking for a way in.

"I have a bad feeling too," Mackenzie said, looking a little scared now. "Maybe someone did hear us shutting the car doors! Maybe the police are already on the way!"

"Guys, relax, okay! We got this. We get in and grab some things that look cool and get out. Simple," JoJo replied, totally calm.

"Really? It's not that simple! It's more complicated than that!" Larry shot back.

"Fine. This was Rachael's idea. How about she takes the lead from here," JoJo shot back.

"Wait? What?" I asked, confused.

"You heard me."

"Well, none of this was my plan. I mean, it was, but this isn't playing out as I expected."

"It usually doesn't," Mackenzie said softly.

I just looked at her.

"Okay, so I was thinking we can get back at this guy by breaking into his place. We take some things and leave. I wasn't planning on running into a crazy chicken," I explained. Mackenzie and Larry softly laughed.

"Not funny, guys," JoJo said, almost irritated.

"Seriously, let's haul ass and find a way in," I said.

"Let's do it," JoJo said, rubbing his hands together. Just a few moments later, Mackenzie found something.

"Hey, check this out. It's an egress window! Do you think we can get in through there?"

"Score! Maybe, I mean, it's big enough for us to climb through!" JoJo said, now pumped.

"But they are usually locked from the inside," I pointed out.

"Really? Don't be negative." JoJo smiled. "I got this."

"What does that mean?" Larry asked.

"It means I got this," JoJo replied.

"Okay. Now you're scaring me," Mackenzie said.

"Relax. Everybody, I got this. I just got to grab something I saw by the shed earlier." JoJo walked back toward the shed, and the rest of us huddled close together.

"Do you have any clue what he's going to do?" I asked Larry.

"No. Not a clue."

"Well, that's comforting," Mackenzie said, a little worried. "Seriously though. Maybe we should just go. I have this bad feeling, and I don't like this anymore."

"If we're not gone in the next ten minutes, then we can go. Is that a plan?" Larry asked.

"Sure. I guess."

"Okay. We're so close now," Larry replied, trying to be calm.

Just then, we all turned to see JoJo coming back with something in his hands.

"What is that?" Mackenzie asked.

"Don't tell me you don't know what this is," JoJo said.

"I know what it is, but I hope you're not going to do what I think you're going to do," Mackenzie replied while looking at the brick in JoJo's hands.

"Oh, hell no!" Larry was doing his best to keep his voice low. "Do not throw that brick through that window! That will attract so much attention."

"Did I say I was gonna do that?"

"That's exactly what it looks like."

"Wow, bro." JoJo chuckled. "Well, okay then." Then JoJo raised his hand in the air, and before Larry could stop him, JoJo threw the brick.

"Oh shit!" I shouted. I couldn't help it as we all watched the brick fly through the air and shatter the window. The sound of the breaking glass was so loud that it was bound to attract attention. Unwanted attention, that is.

"What the fuck did you just do?" Larry shouted, grabbing JoJo's arm. JoJo just laughed.

"Oh my god," Mackenzie said with her hand over her mouth. She then grabbed my arm.

"We gotta hide now!"

"What? Where?"

"The shed." She and I ran fast to the shed, leaving JoJo and Larry behind. We opened the doors, stepped into the shed, and shut the doors fast.

"It's pitch-black in here," I said. My voice was shaking now.

"Just don't move. We don't want to hit anything and make more noise."

"No shit. Oh my god. My whole body is shaking right now," I said, trying to keep calm.

"Same here. What the hell was JoJo thinking? What a dumbass!"

"I have no clue." I suddenly heard something. "Oh shit. Be quiet and listen." I heard what sounded like footsteps heading right toward the shed. Then someone knocked on the door, and Mackenzie and I just screamed.

CHAPTER 48

IN THE DARKNESS OF THE shed, I was shaking so badly, and even though I couldn't see Mackenzie, I knew she was too. Then I felt her grab and squeeze my wrist tight. Then the knocking continued. She squeezed my wrist even tighter. We both froze in place.

"I know you're in there. I heard you scream. So you might as well come out." I didn't recognize the voice. All I knew was that it was a male voice.

"Shit." I heard Mackenzie whisper.

"I know," I whispered back.

"This is Officer Derek Clarkson. Open the shed doors and step out slowly."

"Shit!" Mackenzie said a bit louder. "We're screwed!"

I had no clue what to do. This wasn't me. I've never been in this situation before. My heart was racing a mile a minute. I couldn't relax. So I made my decision.

"Okay," I said loud enough for the officer to hear me. "I'm going to open the door."

"Nice and slow," replied Officer Clarkson.

"Okay." So I put my hand on the shed door and slowly started to push it open. Then I noticed a very bright light. I held my hand up to cover my eyes.

"Keep your hands up and slowly step out," Officer Clarkson said, aiming his flashlight right at me.

"Okay. I just can't see. That light is really bright," I said, still covering my eyes.

"I'll help guide you." Then I saw him reach his hand out to me.

"No. I'm okay." Then when I was completely out of the shed, I looked behind me and watched as Mackenzie stepped out of the shed.

When we were about twenty feet away from the shed, Officer Clarkson stopped us.

"Okay, ladies. Stop right there. Turn around and face me." So we did.

"Do you two mind telling me what's going on here?" His tone didn't seem real serious to me.

"Um. See, we can explain," Mackenzie said, totally scared. She turned to face me. I could tell she was asking me for help.

"Well, I'm waiting."

"We decided to stop by to visit our uncle," I said quickly.

"Really? At this time of night?" the officer asked.

"Yeah. We lost track of time," I continued. "We were hoping to surprise him," I lied.

"Right. So why wear all black?"

"It's our favorite color," Mackenzie said quickly, maybe too quickly.

"Is that right?" replied Officer Clarkson. "This whole thing isn't adding up to me."

Mackenzie and I didn't say a word. We could only just stand there frozen. We had just been caught and could only come up with a cheap lie. Of course, he didn't believe us. Why would he?

"Derek? Where are you? I could really use some help!" came a female voice from behind us. Mackenzie and I quickly turned around to see a female officer quickly approaching us. She also had a flashlight. The light was bouncing as if she was running. When she got close enough, she spotted Mackenzie and I.

"Who are they?"

"I found these two young ladies hiding in the shed. I'm pretty sure they know what's going on here."

"I hate to say this, but it may have to wait. I saw two young males enter this house through the egress window!"

What? I thought. Two young males. Larry and JoJo? Why would they go inside the house? I looked at Mackenzie, and she had to be thinking the same thing because she had a look of horror on her face.

"I already called for backup. We really need to move."

"Damn it." Officer Clarkson was now pretty upset. "You two young ladies are damn lucky. I'm going against my gut instinct right now. You're free to go. Just go fast before I change my mind."

Mackenzie and I instantly started running. We ran past the female officer and ran out of the backyard. We just didn't know where we were running to.

CHAPTER 49

"THIS IS SO STUPID. REALLY stupid. Why did we come in here?" Larry had just been pushed into Anthony Scott's basement by JoJo after hearing footsteps approaching the backyard.

"Because, bro, I didn't want to get caught!"

"This was a really stupid move. You do know that, right?" Larry now seemed mad.

"Dude, you heard the footsteps too. Somebody was coming. So don't be mad," JoJo replied.

"It had to be the cops." Larry took a deep breath, trying to calm down.

"I think you're right," JoJo started. "Hold on. I think I see something." Larry and JoJo were standing in the dark basement when two bright lights came into the backyard.

"Oh shit," JoJo whispered. He and Larry both got down low, hoping they wouldn't be seen.

One beam of bright light went further into the backyard toward the shed. The other beam of light came closer to the house and came closer to the broken egress window. The light stopped once it hit the broken window.

"I need backup right away at 1603 Winston Lane North. Possible robbery in progress," said a female voice.

"Fuck, bro. Did you hear that?"

"Clear as day, JoJo."

Then the woman seemed to pause for a moment, and then she, too, went further into the backyard and toward the shed.

"We gotta move," JoJo said in a panic.

"Where to, genius? If we climb out the window, she's for sure going to see us," Larry pointed out.

"Then we go upstairs. We can go out the front door."

"Really? It won't be that easy."

"Do you have a better idea?" JoJo asked impatiently.

"Damn it. No, I don't. I just can't think right now."

"Let's just go. I can't see a damn thing though. I don't even know where the stairs are."

"Do you have your cell phone?" Larry asked.

"What?" JoJo sounded confused.

"We need some sort of light. We can use the flashlights on our phones and, if needed, cover the lights if any more cops come back," Larry explained.

"Didn't you just say you couldn't think?" JoJo laughed.

"Just grab your phone and turn on the light." Larry sounded a little irritated.

"Okay, okay." JoJo and Larry both took out their cell phones, turned on the flashlights, and let out screams of horror.

CHAPTER 50

"HOLY SHIT! WHAT THE FUCK!" JoJo was in a full panic and had dropped his phone.

"Sshh! Man, relax!" Larry was fast to grab JoJo's shoulder. "We need to pull ourselves together right now!"

"Oh my god, bro! You screamed too. I was not expecting that!" JoJo was grabbing his chest and taking deep breaths, trying to calm down.

"Same here." Larry and JoJo had both been very freaked out when their flashlights landed on a full-sized stuffed bear in the corner of the basement. Its mouth was open, and its teeth were showing.

"Is this dude a taxidermist?" JoJo asked, stepping closer to the bear now.

"Really? Who cares? We gotta move our asses now!" Larry was close to shouting now. Before JoJo could reply, they both heard voices coming from outside.

"Cover your phone," Larry whispered.

"I dropped my damn phone!"

"Are you serious?"

"I think it fell by the bear." JoJo moved toward the bear, but right then, a light beam came through the egress window.

"Fuck." JoJo hid by the bear and was unsure where Larry had gone.

"I heard screams coming from the basement," said a female voice.

"So did I. Can you see anyone?" replied a male voice. Now two flashlights were being shown into the basement.

"I'm not seeing anyone."

"Son of a bitch."

"Maybe they went upstairs," said the male.

"Let's check it out."

After a few moments, the man and woman left. Then it was quiet again. After a few minutes, JoJo called out for Larry.

"Yo, bro? Where are you?"

"I'm over here," Larry called back from the other side of the basement. "I hid under a desk."

"Nice move. I still can't find my phone. Bring your light over here."

"Damn, dude. I'm coming. We gotta find it fast." Larry quickly made his way over to JoJo and started to look for JoJo's phone.

"There! It's right there." Larry pointed toward the bear. "It's between the bear's feet."

"Nice." JoJo was excited and quickly grabbed his phone. "So now what?"

"I don't know. I feel like we're trapped in this damn house."

"Oh no. Do you hear that?" JoJo asked in a panic. Larry and JoJo stayed real quiet and listened to the outside noise. They clearly heard cars pulling into the driveway and doors opening and closing. They also heard voices but couldn't make out what they were saying.

"It's more cops, bro! Oh shit! We're so screwed."

"Fuck! We need to whisper okay and try to calm down," Larry said.

"How exactly do we do that?"

"Dude. I don't know. Maybe try to take deep breaths," Larry suggested.

"You can try that. I gotta get out of here." JoJo aimed his flashlight around the basement, only seeing the stairs going upstairs and the broken egress window.

"There's the stairs, but I don't think we can go up there. The cops will get us for sure, but there's also the window."

"What are you thinking? That the window is our only way out?"

"Yup. Pretty much."

"Crap." Larry took a deep breath. "I think you're right. We need to be very cautious and very quiet. We cannot use our phones. Got it?"

"Got it," JoJo replied.

"First, we gotta see if anyone is out there." Larry put his phone in his pocket and slowly walked toward the window. He looked outside and didn't see any cops in the backyard. He took a risk and slowly crawled into the window.

"What are you doing?" JoJo came closer.

"Sshh. I'm not seeing anyone. Just follow me. This might be our chance to leave." Larry continued to slowly crawl into the egress window. He made his way outside. Then he motioned for JoJo to follow him. JoJo crawled out the window slowly and didn't make a sound. Larry and JoJo were now back in the backyard. They could see blue and red lights coming from the police cars. They could make out voices, but the voices didn't seem to be close to them.

"Now what?" JoJo whispered. Before Larry could answer, a very bright light was shown on his face.

"Police! Freeze! You're both under arrest!"

CHAPTER 51

MACKENZIE AND I RAN STRAIGHT toward Larry's car right after the cop let us go. But now we were slowly walking down the dark street. We figured it would be too suspicious for us to stay by the car. The risk of getting caught again was way too high.

"Oh my god! Look!" Mackenzie was pointing down the street.

"Oh no! That's not good!" I was starting to panic as two police cars were coming right toward us. They had the blue and red lights on but no sirens. They got closer and closer and then just drove right past us. Mackenzie and I turned and watched as they headed toward Anthony Scott's house.

"Oh no! Larry and JoJo! They could get caught!" Mackenzie was in a panic. "There's no way they can escape that many cops!"

"I know! It's all my fault too! It was my idea, and we had bad feelings, and we just didn't leave!" I fell into the grass on someone's lawn and put my hands over my face. Mackenzie sat down next to me and put her arm around my shoulders.

"It's not your fault. We all agreed to this. I don't blame you for anything," she said.

"I blame me. I just had to do this, and it was stupid. I know, and now look." I was starting to cry as I pointed down the street toward the police cars.

"Hey. We all knew the risk, even if we didn't talk about it. We knew. I really hope Larry and JoJo got out of there," Mackenzie said, looking down the street. We both just sat there. We didn't talk anymore. I didn't know what else to say. We could only sit and watch things unfold from a distance and hope that our two friends would be okay.

CHAPTER 52

"PUT YOUR HANDS UP AND don't move!" Emily shouted. It had been Emily's idea for her and Derek to hide in the dark by the shed and to keep an eye on the egress window. She was hoping the two suspects would come out through the window if they thought the backyard was clear. She had been right. Now things were about to take a turn. It was something she never saw coming. She had her right hand on her gun, and her left hand was holding her flashlight, which was now aimed at the two suspects.

"Okay. We're not moving," said one suspect.

Derek stepped forward toward the suspect who had just spoken. He also had his flashlight aimed at him.

"Keep your hands up. What's your name?" Derek asked.

"JoJo. My name is JoJo Winters."

"Okay, JoJo. Why don't you step over here with me." Derek directed JoJo over toward the driveway, toward the police cars.

"Okay. Whatever you say, Officer." Derek looked behind him to see if Emily was following him, but she wasn't.

"Emily? Is everything all right?"

"No. No, it's not." Emily knew who the second suspect was. She just didn't want to believe it. Not until he spoke.

"Hey, Mom," Larry said.

CHAPTER 53

"OH MY GOD!" EMILY WAS shocked. "What are you doing here? I mean, why would you be involved in something like this?"

"It's not what you think," Larry said calmly.

"Then what is it?"

"It was just a joke. I mean, the guy who lives here is a joke," Larry said.

"I know all about him. I just don't know how you do."

"Is this the place to be talking about this?" Larry asked.

"No. Let's go to the car. You can once again get a ride to the police station. Now let's go." Emily motioned for Larry to start walking. They both walked in silence until they arrived at the police car.

"Is that your…" Derek started to ask Emily.

"Yup."

"Um, wow!" Derek was in total shock. "Well, I put JoJo in the back of my car. Do you want Larry back there too?"

"Sure. Why not?" Derek moved fast to open the back door and watched as his partner put her own son into the back of the police car. Again. Once Larry sat down, Derek shut the door and then looked at Emily. She looked like she was about to cry.

"I'm so sorry. If you need some time before we go, just let me know."

"Okay. Just tell the other officers we got the suspects and that they can go," Emily said, trying to pull herself together.

"Okay," Derek said softly and went to speak to the other officers who were at the front of the house.

Emily stood by the car for a few moments while she tried to collect herself. She wanted to remain professional, which meant that she had to stay strong. She couldn't let her emotions control her.

"What the hell is happening?" she said to herself. Then she took a deep breath and got inside the passenger side of the police car.

"Like I said, Mom, it's not what you think," Larry said calmly.

"Let's just have this conversation at the station. Then you both can explain yourselves."

"Wait a minute. I thought you looked familiar," JoJo said to Emily.

"Shut up!" Larry half shouted to JoJo. Emily now turned toward JoJo, who was sitting behind the driver's seat.

"What do you mean?"

"Oh. You came to Speedway to ask questions about the robbery," JoJo replied.

"You dumb bastard," Larry said in frustration.

"Well, this just took another turn," Emily said, turning forward. "Things just keep getting better and better."

CHAPTER 54

"I FEEL LIKE WE NEED to do something. I just don't know what."
I was under a lot of stress. I had no clue what happened to Larry and
JoJo, and I just couldn't relax. Mackenzie and I had decided to call an
Uber and come to my house. We were now sitting on my bed, trying
to wrap our heads around what happened.

"There's nothing we can do. I really hate to say that too."
Mackenzie was scared and couldn't relax either.

"So what now? Do we wait for a text or phone call from one of
them?" My voice was shaky.

"Maybe. I mean, I honestly don't know," she started. "Maybe
what we need is sleep. It's really late. If we can, then we'll be relaxed,
and we can think straight."

"I don't know if I can sleep. My adrenaline is pumping right
now."

"Oh, I get it. Mine too. Let's just lie down then and just breathe,"
she replied.

"I can try. It might help." So I lay down on my bed, and so did
Mackenzie. We were both silent. After some time passed, I could tell
that she had fallen asleep. I just couldn't fall asleep. Not now. I had
so much going through my mind that I couldn't think straight. Two
of my friends could be in trouble. All because of me. I should have
told someone about the way I felt. It's too late now. Would that have
changed things? Maybe. There was nothing I could do now. Just wait
until I hear from one of them if I hear from one of them.

125

CHAPTER 55

EMILY AND DEREK HAD ARRIVED at the police station. Derek was escorting JoJo while Emily was escorting Larry. They had walked into an interview room. Emily was hoping for a private conversation but knew that there was a camera recording everything from the corner of the room. So much for privacy.

They were now sitting at a table in the center of the interview room. Derek was sitting across from JoJo, and Emily was sitting across from Larry. They were all quiet. Emily knew someone had to start talking.

"So? Who's going to speak up first?" she asked in a stern voice. Larry and JoJo exchanged nervous looks.

"Well, where do you want me to start?" JoJo asked.

"From the beginning," Derek replied.

"That could take a while. I mean, if you want the full version," JoJo said.

"We have plenty of time," Emily said. "So the full version it is."

So JoJo started from the very beginning. He knew they were in deep trouble and that it would be best to cooperate. It could possibly help them in the long run.

He said he had a friend who wanted to do something crazy who wasn't trying to hurt anybody. Only that his friend was kind of a rebel. Then he explained everything, how it had been his idea to go to Mr. Scott's house, how they were neighbors, that he knew the type of man Mr. Scott was.

"Okay. Well, that explains how you know about him," Emily said to Larry.

"Yup." Larry had been quiet while JoJo had been explaining things.

"Do you have anything to add?" Emily asked Larry.

"JoJo basically covered it all. He mentioned how our friends were involved. I mean, they didn't go in the house. You know the rest," he said, crossing his arms.

"Okay. Well, breaking and entering is a crime. You both are well aware of that, right?" Emily asked, looking at Larry and then at JoJo.

"Yeah, I know," JoJo mumbled.

"Yup," Larry replied.

"We can't let this slide," Derek said.

"He's right," Emily started. "Since you're first-time offenders, your punishment may not be so bad."

"What? Punishment? We didn't take anything or hurt anyone!" JoJo said in a panic.

"We understand that, but you still broke into a private residence. You broke a window. You need to take responsibility for your actions," Derek replied.

"I can't go to jail! I don't want a record!" JoJo was still in a panic.

"It's too bad you didn't think about that sooner," Emily said.

"Oh, man!" JoJo put his head in his hands.

"I have a question to ask you, JoJo," Emily said.

"Now what?"

"What do you know about the Speedway robbery?"

CHAPTER 56

EMILY WAS SITTING BACK AT her desk with a cup of coffee. It had been a long night. She never imagined that she would be interrogating her own son. Let alone punish him. She had done her best to think and act as a cop. She thought it would make things easier. She was wrong. She knew Larry and JoJo had to be punished. She didn't want them to become repeat offenders. She could make them pay fines or maybe do community service. But she knew she wasn't the one who would decide the punishment. That decision would come from the court.

"Hey. Good morning," Derek said, walking up to Emily.

"Good morning? What time is it?"

"It's 6:10 a.m. I could go to bed right now," Derek said, yawning.

"I'm with you there. So how are Larry and JoJo?"

"Well, JoJo settled down. He actually fell asleep. Larry is just quiet. They're both still in the interview room."

"Okay. Well, that's good."

"What are you thinking?" Derek asked.

"I'm hoping that they don't do jail time. They're first-time offenders. Yes, I know they need to be punished. Maybe they could get court-ordered community service."

"I agree with you there," Derek started. "So do we let them go?"

"I think we should. I'll call Larry's dad. He will need to keep him home. That's going to be a fun conversation," Emily sighed.

"I'm sorry," Derek said softly. "But JoJo did talk about the Speedway robbery."

"He did, didn't he? He wasn't involved in it though. He did say his boss and coworkers all knew about it. That it was funny."

"He also said that the ladies reminded him of his friends."

"True," Emily said. "He chose his words carefully. He knows more than what he said."

"I agree there."

"I need to push that aside and call Larry's dad. I need to get that over with."

"Good luck."

"Thanks."

"I'll make calls of my own. I hope they only get that community service," Derek said, walking away and leaving Emily on her own.

CHAPTER 57

"DUDE, WAKE UP!" LARRY WAS lightly slapping JoJo on the face.

"What? I didn't do it!"

"Huh?"

"I'm out of it. I say weird things when people wake me up, okay, bro," JoJo said, rubbing his eyes.

"I guess. So now what? Are they going to read us our rights?" Larry said, sounding stressed.

"Don't say that, dude! They gotta let us go. Right?"

"I have no clue."

Just then, there was a knock at the door.

"Oh shit," JoJo said, standing up, fully alert. Officer Clarkson slowly walked in.

"How are you guys doing?"

"Um, okay, I guess," JoJo said.

"Can we go?" Larry asked.

"Well, actually, yes. Just one thing first."

"What?" Larry asked, annoyed.

"Well, Larry, your mom called your dad and told him everything," Officer Clarkson said.

"Are you serious?" Larry shouted.

"Just relax. She had to call him. She didn't like it. Your dad isn't happy either. We will let you go home, but you need to stay home. I hope you understand."

"Oh my god! Ugh! Okay, fine. Whatever. Why are you telling me this?" Larry asked, annoyed.

"I'm doing this as a favor to your mom. This isn't easy for her," Derek responded.

"Right," Larry started. "Can we go?"

"You can, yes. Go ahead."

"And JoJo?"

"Well, JoJo. I called your parents. They couldn't believe that you would do this. They said this isn't you. They asked if we could keep you here longer."

"What? Well, are you?" JoJo was in a panic again.

"No, we are not. I told them that you may get community service. They seemed happy with that."

"What? Community service? Are you serious?"

"It's better than jail time," Officer Clarkson replied.

"I'll take the community service, bro."

"I thought so." Officer Clarkson looked at Larry. "You would get it also."

"I figured. So can we both go now?" Larry asked, irritated.

"Yes. Just so you know, Larry, your car is home. I think your dad drove it home."

"That's cool. Gotta go." Larry shoved his way past Officer Clarkson. "Coming, JoJo?"

"Oh yeah." JoJo and Larry walked right out of the interview room. Officer Clarkson just watched them go.

CHAPTER 58

IT'S BEEN THREE WEEKS SINCE our failed crime. I mean, we never really got back at the guy like JoJo was hoping, but we did piss him off. When Mr. Scott saw that his egress window was broken, he called the police right away. I know this because Mr. Scott wanted whoever broke his window to do time in prison. He spoke with Larry's mom, who called Larry. Larry passed the info on to the rest of us.

JoJo and Larry did get community service. Neither one of them said how many hours they needed to serve. They just wanted to keep that to themselves. I still feel it's my fault, even though JoJo and Larry both told me it's not. It's kind of hard to move on.

I did answer Larry's question. I now have my first boyfriend. I couldn't be happier. It is hard to see him. He's either working or doing community service. I know we will make things work.

I haven't seen much of JoJo. He's either working with Larry or doing his community service. I do text him. He says community service sucks. He makes it sound like hell, but I wouldn't know. Overall, he's staying busy and seems happy. He doesn't have any crime plans as of yet. I feel like he just might soon. I could be wrong.

Mackenzie is getting ready for college. Part of her doesn't want to go, but part of her can't wait. She's going to have her own apartment. Just like she planned, it will be right next to the college. She was one of the lucky ones who got an apartment. She has a lot of things already packed and ready to go. So do I. We are still doing my first crazy plan. I will be staying with her. I won't actually be attending college quite yet. I plan on taking a year off. I plan on getting a job too. If my parents ask any questions, I'll just tell them what Mackenzie is doing so it sounds legit. I hate lying. I really do. This is my life. Not theirs. This is what I want.

Larry and I have discussed this. He first laughed at it. Now he understands. We will see each other as much as possible. We will only be an hour apart. This will work out. I know it will.

What about the money in Larry's attic? We took care of that. Mackenzie and I split it since she and I pulled off the robbery. We did offer some to Larry for playing his part and for protecting it for us. He said no. He was satisfied that his boss got what was coming to him.

"So what happens now?" Mackenzie asked. She and I were in my room. She was helping me pack some things.

"What do you mean?"

"Well, we're splitting up. JoJo and Larry will be here, and you and I will be an hour away."

"We'll be fine. We'll all stay in touch and hang out." I smiled.

"I hope so."

"Besides, we need to meet up to plan our next crime," I said, laughing.

"You are totally crazy! You know that, right?"

"Aren't we all?"

ABOUT THE AUTHOR

THE CREW IS THE FIRST published book by Melissa Harman. Melissa loves reading so much that she decided to give writing a try. Melissa currently lives in Minnesota.

Printed in the USA
CPSIA information can be obtained
at www.ICGtesting.com
JSHW022117081024
71077JS00002B/32